Tanglefoot

It was a long way from Kansas to Las Palmas, New Mexico Territory, but Chad Dempster had trouble brewing at home and was hoping the trip would be worth it. He wanted a new town, new ways, and a new name. On emerging from the Overland stage, he got all three at once, but not in the way he could have expected. He stumbled out, hit the ground and became the immediate butt of the local wits who dubbed him 'Tanglefoot'.

Fortunately, or so he thought, Glen Walker, one of the town's first citizens came to his aid, dusted him off and offered him work. What Chad could not have known was that Walker had chosen him as the ideal dupe to help him loot the town of Las Palmas, using a badge and a gun.

Tanglefoot

Logan Winters

A Black Horse Western

ROBERT HALE · LONDON

© Logan Winters 2012
First published in Great Britain 2012

ISBN 978-0-7090-9760-0

Robert Hale Limited
Clerkenwell House
Clerkenwell Green
London EC1R 0HT

www.halebooks.com

Typeset by
Derek Doyle & Associates, Shaw Heath
Printed and bound in Great Britain by
CPI Antony Rowe, Chippenham and Eastbourne

ONE

Glen Walker didn't pay much attention to the stagecoach as it swung into the Las Palmas depot on that sun-drenched New Mexico day. It didn't make much difference to him who came or went. The town always remained the same – dusty-white, lazy, seemingly weary to its bones and yet quite dangerous. Walker could not have cared less about the new arrivals unless they appeared to be someone who might have business with him, or a lady with a well-turned ankle.

He tugged his hat down further as the Overland stage braked to a stop in front of the plastered-adobe building and the trailing dust filtered past. Along the plankwalk more-interested spectators watched the new arrivals. The first passenger disembarking from the coach caught his ignominious nickname in that moment. The young, slender man caught the heel of his boot behind the iron rail of the coach step, fell onto his face in the center of the street, and someone called out:

'Hey, Tanglefoot!'

The chuckling was nearly unanimous. It didn't take much to amuse the local wits.

It was funny enough as far as it went, but there is always someone who decides to take a joke too far. As Glen Walker watched with hooded eyes half-closed against the glare of the white day, Domino Jones walked toward the fallen young man, hitching up his belt. The whiskered Jones winked broadly at the other onlookers and bent over the newcomer.

'Help you up, mister?' Domino asked.

'Sure, thanks.'

Domino dusted off the front of the stranger's coat with his thick hands and said, 'Sorry to intro-duce you to Las Palmas like that.'

'It's all right,' the young man said. He was slightly flushed as he studied the group around him. Again he muttered, 'All right,' and started away. Domino stuck out a boot and tripped him. The crowd roared again with taunting laughter.

'Now he's all dirty again, Domino. Needs a bath! Why don't you help him out? There's the horse trough.'

A quiet voice interjected, 'Why don't you just leave him alone instead?'

Domino Jones wheeled angrily, his beefy face set in a scowl. When he saw who had spoken his fists

6

uncurled and his mouth relaxed into an appeasing smile.

'I didn't know he was a friend of yours, Walker.'

'He isn't,' Glen Walker replied. 'But the man's obviously had a long trip and we can't be welcoming folks to Las Palmas with rough manners.'

'No.' Domino Jones tilted his greasy hat back from his red forehead. His forced smile was still set although his glowering eyes revealed a different humor. Those eyes swept over the sleekly-built tall man in the pressed white shirt and black trousers, impeccably shined boots, gunbelt riding low on his hips. 'I guess you're right, Walker. You know we were just having a little fun.'

'Sure,' Walker said, his amiability easy and transparent. He did not offer to help the young man struggling to his feet. His right hand hovered negligently over the butt of his walnut-gripped Colt .44 revolver. There was nothing obvious about it, but Domino knew Glen Walker well enough not to mistake the implied menace.

The crowd, gathered to watch the joke, briefly expecting – hoping – for a flare-up of tempers between two of Las Palmas's most renowned citizens, now began to drift away toward the shade of the cantinas. With a sound which could have been interpreted as a growled threat or a grunt of amusement, Domino Jones turned and lumbered away, leaving Walker alone in the empty street with the boyish newcomer.

'A rough town, is it?' the fresh arrival asked, dusting himself off again.

'Rough enough,' Glen Walker answered, his eyes still focused on the bearish back of Domino Jones.

'Well, I thank you,' the young stranger said, extending a hand. 'I wouldn't have wanted to end up in a horse trough . . . though I expect I could use it after three days on the road.' He grinned appealingly. Walker did not return the smile, but shook the young man's hand with his own, which seemed to the stranger to be hewn out of walnut. Lithe, strong, calloused in the way only a Western man's can be.

'My name is Charles Proctor Dempster,' the newcomer said, introducing himself.

'Not in this town it isn't,' Glen Walker replied. 'They've branded you, son. From now on in Las Palmas, they're going to call you "Tanglefoot".' Glen Walker clapped a hand on Dempster's shoulder. 'Come on, Charles, let's get whatever baggage you have, find you a hot meal and a place to bunk.'

'I don't understand you a lot sometimes,' Carmalita said to Glen Walker as the badman stood barechested and freshly shaven, looking out the window of the hotel room they sometimes shared. The slender woman moved to him, slipping her arms around his waist as she kissed his back, her huge black Spanish eyes mysterious and content.

'I know that,' Glen Walker said without taking his gaze from the white expanse of desert beyond the window.

'I mean – what you take that pup in for? This Tangle-footed kid. I know that you helped him with Domino, bought him breakfast and found him a place to stay. Why, Glen Walker!'

Walker turned and brought Carmalita's face up to his own, kissing her deeply. Then he laughed, for no apparent reason, causing her cheeks to burn.

'The pup might be of help to me, Carmalita. Leave the thinking to me. Mind your own business and keep on doing what you do best.'

Well, Charles Dempster was thinking as he sat on the edge of his bed, watching the brilliant sunlight stream through the high narrow window of the adobe house, he had at least made a start. He had managed to trek all of the way from Plainview, Kansas to Las Palmas, New Mexico Territory. He had undergone a humiliating but harmless initiation ceremony, been befriended by someone who was apparently well-respected in the town, been fed and housed comfortably if not magnificently in a small adobe house run by two heavy Spanish ladies, whose cooking skills and devotion to their craft were obvious in the meal he had taken that morning and the constant, spicy scents of better things that promised to come.

That is, Charles felt that he had become a man of the West, one of the last of the truly brave and free men on this earth.

So what if, as Glen Walker had warned him, they continued to call him 'Tanglefoot' for a while? The joke would soon wear out and they would forget. For the time being, it was no different from being called Tex or Lefty or Red or Shorty. Men picked up nicknames. Not many could be bothered to call him Mr Charles Dempster when they met. In time they might call him Charlie or Chad, which he preferred. He would carry the name Tanglefoot for a little while; so what? The sobriquet did not offend him, not if he refused to let it.

He had heard men called worse names.

'Am I going mad!' she asked in a troubled voice. 'Or is it you, Glen?'

'I hope it's neither of us, Carmalita,' Glen Walker said, turning away from the mirror, his partially shaven face set in a frown. 'What's troubling you this morning?'

'I heard over at the store – this falling man. . . .'

'Tanglefoot,' Glen said, returning to his shaving.

'Yes, this Tanglefoot man. They say you have found for him a job driving for the stage company. Isn't that the stage that you told me is transferring funds to the bank in Diablo?'

'It is – if I can believe Samuel Pettit, and he does own the bank, so I think he knows.'

'What is it you want to do, Glen?' Carmalita asked, sagging onto the bed. 'Lose that money and get this Tanglefoot killed at the same time.'

Glen Walker wiped his razor, folded it and washed the remainder of the shaving soap from his face and ear.

'Neither,' he told her, lowering his voice as he walked to her and knelt beside her. 'You have to trust me to run my own business. When will you learn that?' His hand was on her thigh. Her fingers toyed with his dark hair. Beyond the window they could hear a group of young boys screaming as they played at some game. It was Saturday morning; there was no school.

'I know,' Carmalita said with a sigh. 'It is just that sometimes I don't know if you are terrible smart or terrible foolish.'

Glen Walker laughed and got to his feet. 'Sometimes I don't know either,' he admitted.

The day was still yawning when Glen Walker knocked on Chad Dempster's door. Enough hot dust was swirling in the air to indicate that the early risers, the miners and the freighters, were active around town. The rest of Las Palmas was locked behind closed doors; most people would rise only when the heat inside their desert holes became intolerable. Dempster opened the door almost immediately.

'Good morning, Mr Walker.'

' 'Morning, Mr Dempster.' Walker surveyed the dim interior of the adobe house. He caught a glimpse of one of the round-faced sisters who managed the tiny boarding house for him. Which, he did not know. Walker didn't remember either of their names, although they were related to Carmalita. But they kept the property, cheaply purchased by him, clean and saw to the needs of any passing men who might have business with Glen Walker.

'How's your room?' Walker asked, stepping inside without removing his hat.

'Fine,' Chad answered. 'And can these women cook! I thank you for letting me stay here. As soon as I can find work, I'll pay you back, of course.'

'That's what I'm here about,' Walker said, gesturing for Chad to sit down on one of the two Navajo blanket-covered sofas. Walker repositioned his holster slightly and sat opposite Chad.

'What is it?' Chad asked.

'I may have found you a job. Can you handle a four-horse team?'

'I have before. It's been a while.'

'This job takes no unusual skills,' Glen Walker said with a smile. 'I've talked to the stage company. They need to run a special cargo through to Diablo

12

today, and none of the regular drivers is available.' Doubt must have crept into Chad's expression, for Walker held up a soothing hand; his smile deepened. 'The horse team has made the run more than fifty times, Chad. They know where they're going and what's expected of them. All you have to do is keep them under control. Can you do it?'

Chad paused only a moment before he said, with a confidence he did not feel: 'I can do it.' After all, what was he to do: turn down his benefactor the first time he offered him work?

'Good,' Walker said, rising. 'I'm counting on you. The stage will be hitched and ready behind the Main Street stable at ten o'clock.'

'Am I going alone?' Chad asked as the two men walked to the front door of the adobe.

'Just you – there are no passengers to worry about. I told you, this is a special run.'

Chad felt a little hesitant, but he had given his word to the man who had befriended him. The heavy door opened to let a slice of desert glare expose the darkness of the room with stunning brilliance. The two men shook hands on the narrow porch and Glen Walker strode away through the fine white silt of the street.

That was taken care of then.

Now he only had to wait for Domino Jones to make his move, which he certainly would considering the amount of money the stage was carrying, and close the mouse trap with his own band of men. Glen Walker felt that nothing could go wrong with the scheme, but as a cautionary reminder, the words of Carmalita sounded somewhere in the back of his mind.

I don't know if you are terrible smart or terrible foolish.

Whichever, the plan was set. Much could go wrong, but if all went well Glen Walker would have the entire town of Las Palmas in his grip, and that was a good feeling. No more double-dealing with scoundrels like Domino Jones, no slipping out of towns in the dead of night to ride the long desert with a posse on his trail, no bribing his way out of some county jail.

Glen Walker had found the perfect way to promote himself to wealthy respectability. He had only needed to wait for the proper dupe to show up. Now he had one, if ever there was one. Tanglefoot was to be his way to pleasant retirement from the outlaw game. And the dupe would not be hurt, might even be greatly aided.

One thing was certain, Tanglefoot would never be the same man he had been after today's work was done.

TWO

The stagecoach was hitched and ready when Chad Dempster walked there through the suffocating dry heat of the day. He had several concerns in his mind; chief among these was his ability to handle the task. He had driven four-horse teams before – twice – for a flour mill in Kansas, but no one had been struck by his proficiency then.

Also, Chad could not help but wonder why a stagecoach with no passengers would be running on a Sunday. He should have asked Glen Walker a few more questions, but he'd been so anxious not to displease the man that he hadn't. Now, as he approached the building where a stablehand stood holding the team, Chad noticed that there was a man just inside the doors of the stable, a rifle in his hands. Across the dusty alley he spotted another man in the meager shade of a stand of cottonwood trees, also armed with a Winchester.

Glen Walker was there to meet him, handing him a pair of fringed coachman's gauntlets. 'You'll need these,' Walker told him. 'Those reins can tear a man's hands up after a few miles.'

Thanking him, Chad asked the obvious questions.

'Is this a dangerous job? Why the armed guards?' Glen Walker smiled easily and slid his hand around Chad's waist, guiding him toward the box of the stagecoach.

'It's a little risky, like most things,' Walker said, 'that's all. The little bank in Diablo is low on cash money and Sam Pettit, our banker, is transferring some funds to them.' Walker's voice hushed a little. 'That's why I picked you, Mr Charles Dempster – you're an honest man. Some of the regular drivers . . . well, I don't trust them too deeply.'

'Will there be a shotgun rider, then? Or armed guards in the coach?'

'No. Don't look worried, Mr Dempster. That's the reason we're doing it this way – on a Sunday with no passengers. From time to time our coaches have been robbed along the way, but with this an unscheduled, empty coach, no one will be waiting for it, and if it's spotted, they will just assume that it is the coach company shifting coaches and stock to a way station.'

'I see,' Chad said, although he wasn't sure he did, but then he was the new man in town, eager to find work, be trusted, and repay Glen Walker. He climbed into the stagecoach box and waited to be handed the reins.

Glen Walker watched him as he untangled the unfamiliar ball of leather ribbons and fitted them to his fingers. Walker spotted the well-used Colt revolver in the stiff, store-new holster and belt Chad wore and smiled thinly. When Chad indicated he was ready, Walker waved goodbye and turned to watch the stagecoach disappear in a cloud of white dust, Chad driving like he was a man holding on for dear life. Walker shook his head and summoned the two riflemen to his side.

'You boys know what to do, don't you?'

'You told us about five times,' one of the men, a stiff-faced thin man answered.

'Then get to it,' Walker ordered.

'This seems like a pretty roundabout way of doing things,' the thin man muttered, drawing a scowl to Glen Walker's face.

'Just do it,' he commanded them. 'It'll pay off later in ways you can't imagine.' Shrugging, the two riflemen walked away to join the others who were holding their horses in the cottonwood grove.

The horses were tough to handle for Dempster. They cleared the outskirts of town and struck out across the long sagebrush stippled flats at a dead run. Walker had told him that the horses knew the way, but it wouldn't do to let them have their heads and run flat out across the desert. He wasn't going to arrive at Diablo with a sweating, foundering team – not on his first job. It took some adjusting of the reins, some more struggling against the animals, a lot of grinding his teeth and cursing, but eventually he managed to settle the horses into a steady, ground-devouring, trot.

The land was long and white, stretching toward the low line of chocolate-colored hills far away. The sky was the palest of blues with sheer puffball clouds scattered across it. It was hot.

Ahead in the road then, Chad spotted the small, indistinct figure of a man standing. There was a saddle at his feet, a rifle in his hand. Chad's first thought was of trouble, but he could see for miles around. The man was alone on the bleak and searing desert. He saw the man's head come up, saw him looking hopefully at the oncoming stagecoach. What was there to do? Chad could imagine himself being stranded on the desert without a horse or water, and he began slowing the team.

'Thanks, friend,' the stranger said, struggling to toss his saddle onto the luggage rack behind Chad. 'I was just slowly baking to death out here.' He clambered up onto the stage seat beside Chad, and they looked each other over. The stranger, Chad saw, was tall, blue-eyed, dark-haired and seemed to be well set-up. His shoulders filled his shirt well. He smiled, showing pleasant white teeth and offered his hand.

'Byron Starr's the name.'

'Chad Dempster. Glad to meet you, I'm only going as far as Diablo.'

'Never heard of it, but if they've got water, that's a place I wouldn't mind seeing.'

'Here,' Chad said, handing him the canteen which had been hanging from a hook on the coach's side. 'This ought to help some. Lost your horse, did you?' Chad asked as he started the team on once again.

'Yes. I should have known better – she was too pretty to last long.'

Chad wondered if Starr was talking about a horse, but it didn't matter. He had other things to occupy his mind. Once the horses had regained their steady pace, Chad said uneasily to Starr:

'I'm really not supposed to pick anybody up.'

'No, I realize that. I sure am glad you did, though,' the likeable young man said. 'I didn't expect to see a stage on a Sunday.' He glanced back, although he could not see the interior of the coach. 'I see you're running empty.'

'Yes.' Chad had practised his lie. 'The Diablo station is in need of a new coach and stock. Something must have happened over there.'

Starr nodded, tilted his hat down against the sun and folded his arms as the rocking stage rolled on. Ahead, through the white glare of the desert day,

Chad could see that the land rose a little. On top of the knoll ahead stood a lone pine tree, strangely out of place against the rock and sand spread around it. For a moment he thought he saw a man on horseback there, moving against the shimmering distances, but when he looked again, the shadowy figure had disappeared. The desert sun can play tricks on the eye.

Chad slowed the team for the ascent, not wanting the horses to labor too hard through the heat of the day. Beside the trail now, on either side, vast patches of nopal cactus grew. If the sketchy instructions he had received were correct, he had only two miles or so to go before he reached Diablo. He should be able to see the town from the crest of the knoll.

They didn't get that far before men burst from the tangle of cactus and the shooting began. The first shot rang off the ironwork of the stagecoach. Starr was instantly alert, aware of what was happening. He shouldered his rifle and shot the man dead. The bullet flung him back into the cactus, his arms flailing as he fell.

Another bullet flew past Chad's ear and almost simultaneously a second was fired. Chad saw a man stand from behind his screen of nopal, swivel his head in confusion, buckle up and die. Chad had not fired, nor had Starr. At least he did not think Starr had. Now his companion had his rifle sighted on a third attacker and, as the coach jolted and lurched over a large rock in the road, he triggered off. Starr cursed under his breath, believing he had missed his mark, but the bandit managed to run away in the direction of the lone pine, dragging his leg before he collapsed.

'Whip those horses!' Starr shouted out, turning on the seat to swing his gun barrel back in the direction of the raiders. Chad could not yank the whip free of its holder, but it made no difference. The horses, frightened by the gunfire, had bolted wildly, and crested the knoll at a dead run as the stage jounced, skidded, and slewed down the slope beyond, racing madly toward Diablo.

Chad heard the sharp crack of Starr's rifle being fired once more beside him, but he did not pause to glance back. The team was out of his control now, and he was just trying to hold the reins and keep his seat in the box. Far away against the gray blanket of the desert floor he spotted the group of tiny buildings which had to be Diablo. Chad hung on for dear life, straining at the reins, hoping the horses would soon run themselves out.

Which they did, another mile or so on. Weary, they staggered across the flats, sweating and unsteady. In just the condition Chad had hoped not to deliver them. He touched his forehead with his gauntlet and wiped back his hair. Starr, who had been watching their backtrail, now settled back into his seat beside Chad, grinning.

21

'Good job handling those horses,' Starr said.

'Are you kidding! They just took off. All I could do was hope to stay aboard.'

'Well,' Starr drawled as he stretched his legs and repositioned his rifle between his knees, 'it looked pretty good to me, Chad. Hell, we got away, didn't we?'

'Who were they, Starr? Enemies of yours?'

'I haven't been around here long enough to have any enemies – or friends. No, Chad, they wanted the coach, that's for sure.'

'But how could they?' Chad asked, perplexed.

'What's this coach really carrying?' Byron Starr asked. After taking a deep breath, and shrugging mentally, Chad told Starr what the stage had aboard. Starr listened, nodding thoughtfully.

'They didn't send a guard along with you? Seems careless to me.'

'Glen Walker explained that doing so would only alert any outlaws,' Chad said. Starr shook his head. He obviously remained unconvinced.

'If I were you I'd have it out with this Walker when you get back to Las Palmas.'

Chad's face heated some. 'You don't understand, Glen Walker is my friend. He would never do anything to intentionally put me in harm's way. His plan just didn't work out, that's all.'

'All right. I didn't mean to start trouble,' Starr answered. 'It's just that it seems a strange way to go about things to me.'

'I apologize too, Starr. After all, if you hadn't happened to be along, I'd likely be buzzard bait by now.'

'I always knew I was good for something,' Byron Starr said with a chuckle. 'Better slow the team a little more. Let's walk them into town.'

There was a small crowd waiting for them at the stage depot. Prominent among them was a wide, round man with a silver star on his leather vest. His shaded eyes were studying Starr and Chad with suspicion.

As Chad halted the team and a narrow stableman came to take the reins, a small man wearing a derby hat which did not quite separate his bald dome from the fringe of red hair circling his skull above his ears, came forward, rubbing stubby hands together with apparent pleasure.

'Well, well,' he said as Chad stepped down from the coach bench, 'I was hoping you would make it.'

Unfortunately for Chad Dempster, his boot leather slipped on the wheel spoke he was using as a step and, as the smiling little man thrust out a hand in welcome, Chad fell to the ground hard, landing on a knee and a shoulder. The stableman laughed out loud and a few others snickered. The town marshal remained stone-faced, and the welcoming man reacted as if he had somehow caused it.

'Oh, dear!' the man in the derby exclaimed. 'Let me help you up.'

Tanglefoot's face was crimson as he was assisted to his feet and dusted off. The man in the derby continued with what must have been an at least mentally-planned speech. Shaking Chad's hand vigorously he said, 'Welcome to Diablo. My name is Walter Pettit, the owner of the Diablo Bank. You have provided a great service to me and my depositors. Several men reported sounds of gunshots from the direction of Lone Pine, and we knew they were not those of a hunter. Did you have much trouble?'

The coach and team were being led away, and as they cleared his line of vision, Chad caught sight of Byron Starr standing, rifle and saddle in his hands, watching expressionlessly.

'There were a couple of men who wanted to stop us,' Chad said. 'My friend there helped out greatly.'

The banker glanced at Starr but returned his attention quickly to Chad Dempster. 'Well, we certainly thank you,' the banker said. Two men had removed a heavy canvas bag secured with a lock from the coach trunk. 'If you need anything, all you have to do is ask,' the little man went on hurriedly. 'Right now you must be tired and hungry. Why don't you and your friend enjoy a meal on the bank over at the Shadyside Restaurant there – it's right across the street.'

'Thank you, sir, that would be a pleasure.' He was

going to add more, but the banker, finished with his formalities, hurried away – presumably toward the bank – with the two men carrying the bag of cash from the stagecoach. The lawman studied Chad and Starr for a minute longer, spat and followed after the banker.

'Glad that's over,' Starr said, looking toward the restaurant. 'I could use a free meal. I don't know about you.'

The two men started that way. Chad was deep in thought. Certain matters about this job seemed very peculiar. He kept his silence until the two were seated at a small square table with a red tablecloth in the corner of the neatly painted white restaurant. A trim little woman took their orders and brought honey and biscuits and a pot of coffee while they waited. Starr had removed his trail worn hat, wiped back his mop of curly dark hair and now proceeded to slather a couple of hot, yeasty biscuits with butter and honey from the beaker on the table. His eyes glowed with satisfaction.

'Am I glad you stopped for me, Chad! Otherwise by now I'd probably be eating mesquite beans and digging a hole in the sand looking for water.'

'Yes, well, you're welcome,' Chad answered. 'You saved my bacon back there.'

'Did I?' Starr looked surprised.

'Sure. I never even drew my weapon. Didn't you notice?'

'There was too much else to look at,' Starr said. He moved his elbows from the table as the waitress returned with their dinners. Both of them had ordered ham steaks, corn on the cob and sweet potatoes. Starr wasted no time in digging in. Chad toyed awhile with his food, cutting his ham, his mind still unsettled.

'Did you hear the banker introduce himself?' Chad asked. 'His name is Pettit – the same name as the banker in Las Palmas. Isn't that a little bit of coincidence?' Starr answered around a mouthful of food:

'I don't think so. Two men with the same backgrounds and education coming West together. They're from some banking family. It's what they know. One tried setting up in Las Palmas, the other in Diablo. Each of them making his way – it makes perfect sense to me.'

'I suppose so,' Chad grumbled, trying the corn on the cob which was dripping rich golden butter. He had another thought: 'How many of those holdup men did you shoot, Starr?'

Starr held up a hand for patience while he swallowed again and drank a little coffee.

'I think I may have gotten two of them,' Starr said after a minute's reflection.

'That was my guess,' Chad replied. 'But I saw at least four of them go down, and I remember hearing other rifles opening up on them.'

'You know,' Starr said after dabbing at his mouth with his napkin, 'I believe you're right about that. It was pretty hot and heavy up there, but it seems to me that there were other guns firing. What can you make of that?'

'Nothing,' Chad told Starr. 'I can't make anything of it at all – but something about this is all wrong, and it makes me think that something in Las Palmas is wrong as well.'

'Well,' Starr said, stuffing another biscuit into his mouth, 'my advice is not to question things when they're going right for you.'

Undoubtedly he was right about that, Chad Dempster thought as they finished their meal and told the waitress to charge it to the Diablo bank, as per Pettit's instructions, but it still gnawed at Chad as they emerged into the heated, cloudless day.

They walked slowly toward the stable beside the way station, where a team of fresh horses was waiting for Chad. The scrawny stablehand approached him shyly and handed him an envelope.

'What's this?' Chad asked. Turning over the heavy manila envelope with its embossed 'Bank of Diablo' in one corner, Chad frowned.

'I dunno,' the stablehand answered uncaringly. 'Maybe a reward or something. I don't open other folks' mail.'

'What is it?' Starr asked as Chad opened the

27

envelope and scanned its contents.

'A letter of commendation,' Chad said with a wry smile. 'It seems I have performed my task bravely and without regard to my personal safety.' He crumpled the envelope and shoved it into his jacket pocket.

'Ah, a hero!' Starr said lightly. 'Don't throw that away, Chad. You said you hadn't yet found steady work in Las Palmas – you'd be surprised how seriously people take a recommendation like that.

'I suppose,' Chad said glumly, 'but I don't deserve it, you know? I was driving in a panic half the way.'

'Who's to know that – or to care? As long as it's down on paper, some folks will take anything seriously.'

'I suppose you're right.' Chad hesitated. 'What about you, Starr? What are you going to do now?'

'I have no idea,' Starr said honestly. 'Right now I have a saddle but no horse. I have a full belly, but no idea where my next meal is coming from. I have no place to go but those I've already been – none of which worked out for me. I don't know. I suppose I'll look around here and see if I can find some kind of work.'

Chad nodded, feelingly. 'How about this, Starr? Do you want to ride back to Las Palmas with me?'

'I can't see that my prospects are any better there,' Starr said. Then his expression cheered, and he reached for the handhold to clamber up into the box, 'But why not? I've nowhere else to go. And at least I'll be traveling with a man of reputation.'

THREE

It was late afternoon when the coach and team driven by Chad Dempster rolled into Las Palmas. Carmalita jabbed a finger into the dozing Glen Walker's ribs as she stood at the window watching. 'Get up. You have to see this,' she said.

Glen Walker sat up grumpily. Carmalita, who was usually content to spend most of her day in bed herself, seldom bothered him when he was asleep. 'What is it?' he asked, frowning as he swung his legs to the side of the bed.

'He is back, the Tangleman.'

'Tanglef . . . Mr Charles Proctor Dempster.'

'Your protégé. How do you say that in English?'

'Dupe,' Walker muttered, still half-asleep. He walked heavily to the window and peered out past the curtains. It was Dempster driving the stage, certainly but who was the man with him? He seemed vaguely familiar, but Walker was sure he was not from Las Palmas. Where had he come from?

'Oh, I did not tell you that my cousin, Candida, arrived this morning. While you were sleeping,' Carmalita said at his elbow.

'Your cousin? How many cousins do you have?'

'I don't know,' Carmalita shrugged. 'Many. We are an affectionate family. She is going to stay with her aunts.'

'You mean over at the place where Tangle . . . Mr Dempster is staying?'

'Yes, those are her aunts, my aunts – you know that.'

'I remember,' Walker said, sitting down on the bed. He rubbed his forehead with the heel of his hand. He didn't like extra people clogging up his plans. Though, what difference could Carmalita's cousin possibly make? Now, the man traveling with Dempster. . . .

'Tell me again, what you told me last night,' Carmalita urged, sitting beside him on the bed. She was only half-dressed and very appealingly so.

'What did I tell you?'

'When you were drunk, you explained the plan to me so that I would understand it all.'

Glen Walker glanced at her, his eyes lingering on her full, lovely figure. 'Did I really tell you all?'

'I don't know if it was all. I sometimes think that you think I am stupid,' Carmalita said with a pout on her full lips.

'Not at all, my darling. I think you are quite clever in your way. But this is all my business.'

'Tell me again,' she pleaded.

'Get me a glass of water; my mouth is bone dry.' When she returned with a glass of water from the pitcher on the counter, he told her. 'I'll tell you again, but you are sworn not to say a word.'

'I am sworn *never,*' Carmalita answered. 'What is good for you is good for me, too, right?'

'That's right – and you'd better not forget that,' Walker said. 'All right,' he began, handing the glass back to her. 'I arranged for Dempster to drive the stage to Diablo. No one was supposed to know about the money transfer. But I did, of course, and Domino Jones found out.'

'How did he find out?' Carmalita asked. Walker only smiled.

'He found out, let's leave it at that. Knowing what was likely to happen, I sent Skinny Jim and a few of the boys out to watch for Domino's crew, and if they saw them trying anything, to make sure they didn't succeed.'

'To ambush them if they tried to ambush Tangle . . . Mr Dempster.'

'That's right, and apparently it worked. Now Dempster is a hero to the folks in Diablo and a hero to Sam Pettit at the bank. He fought off a gang of outlaws and took the money through.'

'I can't see how that works for you,' Carmalita said.

'No? I'll tell you, then. When Las Palmas needs a new town marshal, I mean to propose Mr Charles Dempster for the office.'

'We still have Marshal Cody,' Carmalita objected.

'For now,' Walker replied. 'We have to strike while the memory of Dempster's heroics is fresh in the minds of the citizens. It shouldn't be any problem to get him appointed with Sam Pettit behind him.'

'There is still Marshal Cody,' Carmalita reminded him again.

'Ah, that is the way of life – here today, gone tomorrow.'

'You mean to persuade him to leave Las Palmas?' Carmalita asked, her wide dark eyes perplexed.

'That's it,' Walker said. 'I am going to convince him that he should leave.'

Carmalita rose from the bed, her swaying hips magnetic to Walker's eyes. She bent low to look out of the window again. Her expression had grown puzzled as she turned toward him once more. 'I do not see what we profit from having this Charles Proctor Dempster as town marshal.'

'You don't?' Walker smiled, lay back on the bed with his hands behind his head. With half-closed eyes, he asked, 'How many businesses are there in Las Palmas?'

'How many?' Carmalita's eyebrows drew together. 'Of what kind?'

'Of all kinds.'

'All kinds? Maybe fifty, a hundred. I don't know.'

'How much money do you think they pull in in a month?'

'Altogether, it must be a lot – I don't know.'

'I do. And for too long they've been thriving, with free law enforcement to protect them. From here on out they are going to pay five per cent of their profit to us. It's not enough to make them cause an uproar, but five per cent from every business in town, especially the big saloons, will add up to quite a sum. Anyway,' he shrugged, 'all they have to do is jack up their prices a little to cover the cost.'

'You are a devious man, Glen Walker,' Carmalita said as she lay down to snuggle against him. 'You always said that you would make us rich.' She sat up abruptly, bracing herself on one arm. 'But will Domino Jones stand for it?'

'He may not even ever know. He's not smart, you know. He and the other old-time bandits still only know how to operate in one way – pull your gun and demand a man's money. We're going to make our fortune the new way, the most profitable way. They call it politics. I should be able to convince the mayor and town council that times have changed and we need to do this to protect the town from thieves.'

'You think they will agree?'

'As long as they get their cut. I told you, it's politics; no one minds taking money from the citizens so long as some of it ends up in their fat pockets.'

'You are a sly and greedy person, Glen Walker,' Carmalita said as she snuggled up tightly against him.

'So are you, my darling,' Walker said quietly, 'so are you.'

With the horses and coach given over to the stable crew, Chad made his way home, taking a reluctant Byron Starr along with him.

'I don't know these people, Chad, and I haven't any money.'

'It's all right. My friend Glen Walker owns the house, and the women there are some sort of relations to his girlfriend.'

'If you say so,' Starr replied.

'Sure I do, and wait until you taste the food these women can cook! Pork *tamales, carne asada, chorizo, machaca. . . .'*

'I don't even know what any of that is,' Starr said as they trudged toward the front door of the adobe house.

'You will, my friend and you won't ever forget after you try some.'

The front door stood wide open, which was surprising since usually people in this section of the country kept the doors shut as long as possible to keep out the desert heat. Windows and doors stood wide open after sundown, but not at midday. Chad realized instinctively that something was happening. Starr noticed his expression.

'What is it?'

'I don't know,' Chad had to say. Starr had already dropped the saddle he had been carrying over his shoulder, and now held his rifle in both hands.

'I'm sure it's nothing,' Chad said. 'I'm just a little jumpy after this morning.'

'Having men shoot at you can do that,' Starr agreed. They stepped up onto the porch and went inside the dark house, closing the door behind them. There was the smell of salsa being simmered in the kitchen, and the lingering scent of the old women's powder and soap. No one was moving about the adobe.

'Why don't you take a seat and let me look around,' Chad said, nodding at the sofas with the striped Indian blankets on them.

'If you're still uneasy, I can go with you,' Starr offered.

'No – I have no reason to think anything's wrong. It's just that it hasn't been an easy day for me. I just have some left-over jumpiness.'

'I'll be here,' Starr said, settling on the comfortably upholstered sofa – a rare luxury for a long-traveling man. 'Just scream if you need me.'

Chad was feeling too weary to take offense at the light mockery in Starr's voice. He turned and walked down the dark hallway to his room.

Someone was in there!

He didn't scream, but his throat constricted and he drew his revolver, holding it high beside his ear as he toed the door to the room open. The woman inside was only half-dressed, and she spun toward him, holding her dress up in front of her. Her dark hair was loose around her shoulders; her eyes flashed.

'Who are you in my room?' she shrieked, her voice heavy with a Spanish accent.

'Who are you in my room?' Chad said. He noticed an open suitcase on the bed, and a large trunk standing near by. The window was open, the curtains parted enough for the daylight to reveal a beautiful woman in her late teens or early twenties. She wore a necklace of silver conchos. Chad holstered his weapon and tried for a smile. It was an awkward expression.

'Look,' he said as calmly as he could, 'I've been staying here. In this room.'

'This is the home of my aunts,' the girl answered indignantly. 'You, go away!' The girl's eyes went to the door. 'Tia Margarita,' she said, and Chad shifted his eyes to see one of the little round women standing there, bed linen in her hands. 'Who is this . . . what is he doing in my bedroom?'

'Did you, uh, come back?' the older woman said, obviously having trouble with her English.

37

'Of course,' Chad said patiently. 'No one told me I had to leave. Glen Walker told me I could stay here as long as necessary.'

'Glen Walker?' the young woman said. She had turned her back and was struggling into her pink dress as Aunt Margarita frowned at each of them in turn. 'Glen Walker is. . . .' Candida broke into rapid Spanish which Chad could not follow. Her aunt nodded and shrugged.

When Candida finished her outpouring Margarita poked her fingers into her graying hair and admitted, 'Yes, it is true. This man is an *amigo* of Señor Walker. We thought he was going away this morning. He got on the . . . eh, stagecoach and left.'

'You are a friend of Glen Walker?' the younger woman asked.

'Yes. A good friend.'

'Then you know my cousin, Carmalita.'

'I haven't met her.'

'Then not so good a friend, I think,' the girl said, pushing out her lower lip. 'My name is Candida. As you know, these are my two aunts, Margarita and Rosa,' for the second sister had appeared in the doorway, her round face a mask of confusion.

'I'm Chad Dempster,' he said. 'Look, I didn't mean to cause any trouble. It's just that this room was given to me. I just figured it was still mine – I even brought a friend back to stay with me until he can get on his feet.'

'Your friend,' Candida said. 'Are you sure it is a man?' There was a twinkle in her eyes that both pleased and embarrassed Chad.

'That's what they tell me,' Starr's voice said from the doorway. 'I heard a ruckus back here, Chad, and thought I'd better come and investigate.' His eyes lingered on Candida, 'It seems you have things well in hand.'

'I am so sorry,' Aunt Margarita said. 'Only mistakes. Of course you may have your room, Señor Chad. There are two beds in this room, and so your friend can stay. Candida – we will have to move you.'

'I'm sorry,' Chad said to Candida, but the girl was still smiling with amusement. What exactly it was that she found funny he didn't know.

'It is of no matter – I am the intruder,' she said as she closed the open suitcase and reached for a hairbrush she had left on the bureau. She swept out past Chad, trailing a lavender scent.

Chad asked, 'Do you want me to bring that trunk?'

'Oh, no. You are a guest,' Margarita said, 'Rosa and I can carry it.'

When the women had gone, Starr made his way back into the room, lugging his saddle with him. He dropped this on the floor and stood looking appreciatively around the room. 'This is a nice place, Chad. Remind me to show you the bush I slept under last night.'

Chad grinned and sat on his bed. 'It suits me too. Did you get a whiff of that food cooking in the kitchen?'

'Among other things,' Starr said, seating himself on the opposite bed. 'Man, you have fallen into some good luck, haven't you? Home-cooked meals, a soft bed, a pretty girl interested in you. . . .'

'I don't even know her,' Chad objected.

'No, but she's noticed you, Chad. There are women's smiles and women's smiles. That one she left on you wasn't because she thinks you are an amusing person.'

'That's. . . .' Chad began, but his denial lost its force. Maybe that was because he wished what Starr said were true. Maybe Candida did think he was an interesting man, though why she would was a mystery. But as he stretched out on his bed and tried to make up for lost sleep and the rigors of the trail, he let his imagination linger on the dark-eyed girl and believe just for a few minutes that it might be so.

It was still only mid-afternoon when Chad awoke. Opening his eyes, he saw that Starr was already awake, cleaning and oiling his pistols at the table in the corner of the room. The light in the room was murky, and the afternoon heat had begun to gather. Chad sat up on his bed, wiping the perspiration from his forehead with the back of his hand.

'These thick adobe walls are fine for keeping the morning heat out,' Byron Starr said, snapping the loading gate on his pistol shut and holstering it, 'but I guess nothing can defeat the desert heat all day long. Want to go out and get some fresh air and a cool drink?'

'Yeah,' Chad replied like a dazed man, which he was by heat and sleep. 'The aunts don't serve dinner until hours after dark; another desert custom.' He paused. 'We could grab a beer or two. And I should report back to Glen Walker, anyway.'

Starr rose to his feet, smiling. 'Don't forget to bring your bona fides along with you.'

'My what?'

'That letter you got from the banker in Diablo.'

'Oh, that. I don't think it would impress Walker much.'

'Maybe not, but as I'm sort of riding along on your coat tails right now, it's important to me that you maintain your reputation – after all, we're both unemployed as of now.'

'I suppose you're right,' Chad answered. 'It all seems sort of silly, though.'

'To you, maybe, maybe not to other folks.'

Dan shrugged a response, slipped into a clean blue shirt and stuffed the letter from Walter Pettit into his pocket. Maybe Starr was right about that. It at least showed that he had completed his assignment competently. Whether that was true or not . . . it was Starr, after all, who had pulled them through.

They started toward the front door of the house. Chad caught himself glancing around: he knew whom he was hoping to see, but Candida was nowhere to be found. They swung open the heavy door on its pin-and-iron-ring hinges and went out into the glare and heat of the summer day.

They started walking toward town. Neither man had a horse and no prospect of getting one any time soon. Chad, at least, knew he was due some sort of wages, but he and Walker had not discussed what that amount was to be. The ground underfoot was still only white dust, fine as silt. Each step brought up small puffs of dust. The air was hot, dry and stagnant.

'Do you have any idea where we're going?' Chad asked his cheerful companion.

'I saw a beer parlor when we pulled into town. A place called FitzRoy's, I think it was. We'll cool off for a while, then go track down Glen Walker and see what kind of situation he has in mind for you.'

'If any,' Chad said glumly. His hat was pulled low as they trudged along through the nearly deserted streets of Las Palmas.

'If any,' Starr agreed. 'Then we'll know what we're facing, if we have to make plans to travel on.'

'I don't know if I've got any traveling left in me,' Chad said. His mouth and throat were dry, parched by the sun.

'We can cut through here,' Starr said, pointing out an alley that ran between a blacksmith's shed and a cobbler's shop. The ground there was oily and stank of slag. Chad was only thinking how good a mug of beer would go right now. He glanced up to look for FitzRoy's saloon and saw two men, indistinct shadows in the close alley, standing in front of them.

'Watch it, Starr,' he breathed, and Starr glanced that way.

'Friends of yours?' Starr asked.

'I only know the one by name: the big one. Domino Jones, and he's no friend of mine.'

'What do they want?'

'I'd have to guess, but it's nothing good,' Chad muttered.

As they approached, both of the waiting men spread their feet, bracing themselves. Their hands dangled loosely near their handguns.

'Hey, Tanglefoot!' Domino Jones bellowed. 'I've got something for you.'

Chad and Starr halted, sizing the men up, but it was only seconds later that Jones drew his Colt and drew back the hammer. Chad flailed at his holster, trying to draw his own weapon, but was far too slow. As Jones's companion also drew his gun Chad saw Starr draw with remarkable swiftness and fire three shots at the two of them.

Domino Jones swung around, dropping his gun,

holding his injured arm with his other hand. The second man, slighter, bearded, was not so lucky. One of Starr's bullets took him full in the throat. Where the other shot went was anyone's guess, but it didn't matter. The bearded man lay crumpled up, dead, against the alley floor.

Chad heard Starr curse. There was movement in the blacksmith's shop, and a head peered out. Gun smoke still drifted in the air. 'I must be out of practice,' Starr muttered. 'I was trying to just wound the both of them.'

Chad, who had drawn his gun by now, simply stared as the unarmed Domino Jones fled the scene of the gunfight and the other man, after a moment's reflexive twitching, lay still against the oily alley floor. A few ambitious flies had already settled on him.

'Starr, you're a wonder,' Chad said admiringly.

'Am I?' Starr replied dourly. 'My first day in town, I kill a man I don't even know. What's usually done in these cases?' he asked, looking at the dead man.

'You forget I've only been here a day longer than you,' Chad answered. 'Report it to the town marshal, I expect.'

'All right,' Starr said with a sigh. 'I wish we had a witness or two.'

'The smith saw it,' Chad said, nodding toward the building.

'Did he? I hope so. I don't feel like going to jail,

and I haven't got a pony to escape on. All right,' he sighed again, 'let's turn ourselves in to the law.'

'We'd better,' Chad said.

'If we manage to wriggle out of this, I still mean to have me some beer. I thought I would have two of them, but now . . . I might need a few more than that.'

FOUR

Marshal Ben Cody was a pouched, baggy-eyed man who had a world-defeated expression on his fallen face. He looked as if he had forgotten whatever it was that had drawn him to Las Palmas, and that it was no longer even of importance to him.

'What is it, boys?' he asked as Starr and Chad entered his dry-heated office. He swung his feet to the floor as if it pained him to stir that much.

'Two men tried to mug us,' Chad said.

'We left one of them dead,' Starr chipped in. He was moving around the room, examining the Wanted posters, the map of the territory on the wall.

'Dead,' the marshal said. That meant he would have to move from his chair, which from the look of his nearly 300 pounds, would require a lot of unwelcome effort. 'Who was it that was killed?'

'We didn't know him,' Chad said. 'Two men

braced us with drawn guns. . . .'

The door behind Chad had opened and Glen Walker and the banker, Sam Pettit entered, leaving the door open to the hot glare of the day. Glen Walker spoke up.

'It was Charlie Burnett. He and Domino Jones tried to waylay this man – the two of them,' Walker said, noticing Starr for the first time.

'Domino Jones is over at the doctor's, getting his arm patched up,' Sam Pettit put in. 'These two young, honorable men instead of slinking away have come to the law to explain.'

Marshal Cody who seemed to have a dubious respect for the banker, listened to him and asked, still without rising. 'Any idea why Domino Jones would try to stick up these two?' He looked in turn from Walker to Pettit, to Chad and Starr.

'I do,' Byron Starr said. He plucked the letter of commendation from Chad's pocket, handing it to Glen Walker instead of the lawman. 'I think it had something to do with the robbery attempt out on the Lone Pine road.'

'But, why. . . ?' Marshal Cody asked, not comprehending. Glen Walker interrupted him.

'I'll tell you why,' he said, showing the banker the commendation before tossing it on the marshal's desk. 'It was Domino Jones's gang that tried to hold up that stage. They didn't get the cash, and they meant to take their payment in blood by killing

Charles Dempster here.'

'It's possible, I suppose,' the marshal admitted, studying the letter from the banker in Diablo.

'This young man is a hero,' Sam Pettit said, placing a hand on Chad's shoulder. 'If you won't take my word for it – and that of my brother – why don't we just wait and see if Domino Jones comes to report a crime against him.'

'That'll never happen,' Glen Walker said.

'I was there,' Starr volunteered. 'That's exactly the way everything happened. I'm not sure, but I think the town blacksmith witnessed it, too.'

'You might ask Meyer about the shooting,' the banker said. 'That's not too far for you to walk, is it?' There was a hint of sarcasm in Pettit's voice.

'I'll talk to the smith and see what Domino has to say – if he ever shows up,' Cody said, stretching his huge flaccid arms and rising. 'I can't see any reason to hold these two boys right now, seeing that both you and Walker are vouching for them.'

Cody rose heavily from his chair, grabbed his hat and strolled, or rather, waddled, across the street toward the blacksmith's – Meyer's – shop. Doing that and seeing that Charlie Burnett's remains were disposed of were all that he could do, or was inclined to do, at that point.

'Well, men,' Glen Walker said, 'what do you say we have a talk about your futures – yours especially, Chad? I have plans for you.'

'Do you? I was hoping you might have some idea of how to keep me working,' Chad said. 'And Starr, too, of course.'

'Starr? That's your name is it?'

'That's it,' Byron Starr answered. 'As for any help you could give me, Walker, I'd appreciate it greatly. But for now Chad and I have an appointment to keep over at this FitzRoy place down the street.'

Walker smiled. 'I understand you, Starr. I'd ask to go along with you, but Carmalita has her mind set on going out to dinner, and I never disappoint a lady.'

'We met her cousin,' Chad said as the group of men stepped outside. 'Candida – that's it, isn't it, Starr?'

'You know it is,' Starr said drily.

'I've never met her,' Walker said. 'How is she looking?'

'Fine,' Chad said looking down at the ground. 'She's looking just fine, sir.'

'Does she . . . I hope she doesn't resemble her aunts too much?'

'She weighs about a hundred and ten pounds, and well distributed they are,' Starr said. Chad felt his face redden. Walker grinned.

'I'll report to Carmalita. You boys might see us over at the adobe later for a little family gathering, and for our business chat.'

'That went well enough,' Chad said as they

walked the boardwalks toward FitzRoy's.

'As well as could be expected,' Starr agreed. 'In a lot of towns we would have had to steal ourselves a couple of horses and beat it for the desert.'

'I suppose so. I told you Glen Walker was a good friend.'

Starr was thoughtful for a moment. 'Yes, it seems so, but Chad – what does he do, exactly? Who is he?'

Chad found himself stumped for a moment. 'I don't know exactly. He has some sort of pull in this town, but I don't know him well enough to answer your questions.'

'For the time being,' Starr said cheerfully, 'I don't suppose it matters. I was just wondering.' They had reached the FitzRoy saloon and Starr held the door open for Chad to pass through.

The interior of the saloon was broader than they had expected. There were only a dozen or so men there in this heat, sleeves rolled up, heads hanging down, looking desert-beat although all of the windows had now been opened in anticipation of the evening breeze. They found a table near one of the western windows and ordered a pitcher of beer.

As they settled in to wait for the evening coolness, Starr told tales of his rambling, exciting life. Exaggerated or not, which made no difference to Chad, they were entertaining. As for Chad, he had not much to offer in terms of daring exploits. His life in the Wild West had only begun a day ago, and

Starr had been present at its two most exciting moments – the stage robbery attempt and the shootout with Domino Jones and his friend, in neither of which Chad had actively participated, to be honest. In fact if he had not happened to pick Starr up out on the desert, Chad knew, he would probably be dead by now.

'There's one,' Starr said as he paused to pour himself a fresh glass of beer. The shadows were long outside and merging softly inside the saloon. Chad didn't catch Starr's meaning until he followed his eyes and saw a tall redhead with a full figure leaning against the bar. She wore a red dress with black lace at the cuffs and hem. Starr was gazing that way, his eyes slightly glassy, slightly hungry.

Chad said, 'I prefer them—'

'I know – you prefer them a little fresher, a little younger. But, son, breaking them in is much over-rated, take my word for it. Your Candida, for example, is not my type at all, if I ever gave you cause to concern yourself about that. She's definitely the type a young pup would crave, but not an old dog like me,' said Starr who could not have been more than four or five years older than Chad Dempster – or perhaps he was much older than Chad in terms of experience.

'Excuse me,' Starr said, rising abruptly. 'I think I've just met an old friend I've never seen before.' With that he strolled over to where the redhead was standing and struck up an immediate conversation, which Chad would have found impossible. By the time the beer was gone, Starr and the lady were deep in close communication, her smile bright and luminous, several drinks between them. The man would not be returning to the table, Chad knew.

After half an hour he rose, nodding toward Starr, who did not notice him, and went out into the cool purple twilight of Las Palmas. Chad had had enough beer, enough excitement, and not nearly enough rest. He started on his way home, keeping his eyes on the shadows that lurked in the hidden places.

He thought of stopping for a bite to eat, but why, when there were two superb cooks at the house who enjoyed preparing meals for him? He shuffled slowly toward the house, enjoying the relative coolness of the evening. Only one person passed him, a kid on a plow horse who waved a hand merrily, a hound dog following in his dusty wake. Las Palmas wasn't such a bad town, Chad decided.

A buggy stood in front of the adobe house when he reached it. Lamps burned within. The door and windows had been flung wide, of course. The solitary elm tree in the front yard stood motionless in the breathless night, like a weary, shaggy ghost, black against the starry sky. Chad wiped off his boots on the steps, removed his hat and entered the house. He found Glen Walker standing with his back to the cold fireplace, a short whiskey in his hand. On one of the sofas sat the banker, Sam Pettit. On the facing sofa Candida perched beside a woman who had to be her cousin, Carmalita, wearing a daring dark-blue dress with a plunging neckline.

Glen Walker seemed to be watching her with pride as Chad glanced that way. The two cousins were very much alike, but whereas Carmalita stared back boldly, Candida looked away, seemingly embarrassed by her cousin's costume and the way it caught the men's eyes.

'Glad you made it!' Glen Walker said warmly. 'I was afraid you and your friend might be out making a night of it.'

'That was enough for me,' Chad Dempster said. 'I'm not much for the night life.'

The banker cleared his throat and looked meaningfully at Walker, as though time were being wasted. 'The matter we have come about. . . .' he prompted.

'Yes. Carmalita, why don't you two be good guests and see if the aunts need any help in the kitchen?' Both women, raised in the tradition that men must be left alone to discuss their business, rose and made their way to the kitchen. Glen Walker watched them go, a smile on his handsome face. He turned to Chad.

'Now, then, Mr Dempster, would you like a drink

of whiskey – I guarantee you that is the prime goods. None of that saloon rot.'

'I think not,' Chad said, seating himself where Candida had been sitting. He imagined he could still feel her warmth on the cushion. 'I'm not much of a drinking man.'

'Fine,' Walker said, refilling his own glass from a fancy-looking bottle. 'That's a good recommendation for you.'

A recommendation? For what, Chad wondered?

'Let's get on with it,' Sam Pettit urged, looking at his silver pocket watch. 'I have a meeting with the mayor in less than an hour. I'd like to have this all settled by then.'

'All right, Sam,' Glen Walker replied with a show of chafed patience. He sat down facing Chad and said:

'We want you to be our town marshal, Mr Dempster.'

'You what?' Chad said. He cocked his head like a dog, not sure that he had heard the man clearly.

'We want you for town marshal,' Glen Walker said again. 'You've seen the man who presently holds the job – Ben Cody. He no longer has the ability or the willingness to perform his duties in a satisfactory manner. Is that your judgement as well, Pettit?' Pettit nodded emphatically yet doubtfully.

'The job is yours,' the banker told Chad with the same hint of doubtfulness in his voice.

Chad rose to his feet and spread his arms, 'I thank you men . . . but I have no experience as a lawman, no knowledge of the town codes, I'm not much of a gun hand.'

'You can learn as you go along,' Glen Walker said smoothly. 'That's the way we all learn our jobs, is it not?'

'We just need someone who is eager to do the job well,' Pettit put in. 'You've already demonstrated your willingness and ability – after all you did take the cash transfer through to Diablo despite being attacked along the way. Right here in Las Palmas, you managed to take care of two of our local toughs as they tried to do you harm – Domino Jones and Charlie Burnett. You have what it takes, son.'

'Do I?' Chad said, not quite aloud. He knew that his performance in the episodes mentioned had not been as glorious as a simple reading of the reports might indicate. Raising his voice, he told the two men, 'I hate to take another man's livelihood away from him.'

'Cody?' Glen Walker laughed. 'He'd likely be relieved to find out that he will no longer have to drag himself out of bed in the morning. He'll have a small pension, Chad. Enough to get by on.'

'Not that lazy Deke!' the banker protested.

'No, of course not. He's able-bodied.' To Chad who did not know who they were talking about, he explained. 'Deke, Deacon Forge, is Ben Cody's nephew and the deputy marshal. He'll probably be just as relieved as Ben Cody. It will mean he won't have to cut his nights spent gambling at the Clipper saloon short so that he can get a few hours' sleep before he goes on duty.'

'You will need a deputy,' Sam Pettit told Chad. 'What about that young friend of yours? He seems to be a cool customer.'

'Starr?' Chad's head was reeling. This was all happening just a bit too fast for him. 'I can ask him, but I don't know if he would be interested.'

'Is he in a hurry to get somewhere? Another job waiting for him?' Glen Walker asked. At the shake of Chad's head, Walker said, 'He'll be interested, then. It's a good spot for a man. Long-term employment. If you don't want to take him on,' Walker added with a shrug, 'that's up to you, but it seems to me folks are generally happiest working with people they already know.'

They both seemed to have assumed that Chad had accepted their offer. He supposed he had. He was through with traveling. He had made his way to Las Palmas and meant to stay for a while – he saw Candida's shadowy form pass the doorway, carrying a platter. She was enough reason to try it for a while. And he was still obligated to Glen Walker. With nowhere else to go, with no money, what better opportunity was likely to come up? And he could help out Byron Starr at the same time. The truth was, he would feel safer, more sure of himself with a man like Starr at his side. Everyone who was a lawman had to have his first day on the job, and he had no other skills. Only his quiet ambition to be someone . . . Candida crossed the doorway again . . . someone respectable.

'All right. I'm your man,' he told Glen Walker.

Chad Dempster awoke slowly the following morning. The coolness of the room bordered on being chilly. He sat up groggily, rubbing his head. Glancing at the bed across the room, he saw that Starr had not made it home the night before. He had not really expected that he would.

As Chad rose, yawning, to his feet, a surge of excitement began to bubble up inside of him. He was a working man! Not only that, he was to be the town marshal of Las Palmas. Most of his doubts and fears were washed away with that sudden awareness. Or had he imagined it, dreamed it?

No. He sat on his bed again and reviewed the conversation he had had with Glen Walker and Sam Pettit the night before. All that was needed was the mayor's approval, and Pettit seemed to feel that that was in the bag. Pettit's opinion carried a lot of weight in this town as the guardian of the purse strings.

Chad dressed, whistling as he stepped into his pants, slipped his shirt on and buttoned it up before closing the window to his room in deference to the local habit of keeping the cool of night locked down within the adobe houses for as long as possible. He washed his face in the basin provided and sniffed the air. The aunts would already be up and cooking. Now was the time of day to do that, before the angry sun crested the horizon.

There was a light tap on his door, causing Chad's head to swivel that way. He thought that it must be Starr returning, shamefaced, but Starr was not the sort to rap gently. He would have simply swung the door wide and entered. Frowning, Chad went to the door, and swung it inward.

'I am sorry – I must talk to you,' Candida said in a whispery tone of voice. 'I know it is early, but I heard you moving about.' Her dark hair was loose around her shoulders, brushed to a high gloss, and she wore a nightdress and wrapper. She was barefoot.

'What is it?' Chad asked with some alarm. There was fear in the girl's eyes.

'Let me come in,' Candida said, 'and shut the door behind me. It is my cousin, Carmalita and her friend. She tells me all; she and I are like sisters. . . .'

'Come in and tell me,' Chad said, frowning. Despite her general lack of a heavy accent, she pronounced the word sisters as 'seesters', something Chad found charming in an indefinable way. Candida was charming in other ways that could be well-defined. Smooth skin, shiny dark hair, well-formed petite body and large Spanish eyes ... unhappy Spanish eyes.

'Sit down,' Chad gestured. Candida glanced at the bed, back at the wooden chair which stood in the corner and took the chair, sitting there with her hands folded on her lap, her face turned down. There might have been the sparkle of a tear in the corner of one of her eyes.

'What is it, Candida?'

Her eyes were huge and sad as she looked up at him through the shadowed morning light.

'It is this man, this Glen Walker,' she told him. 'I think you must run away from Las Palmas. Now! Or you will have to kill him.'

FIVE

Studying the girl who sat in his bedroom, Chad could see the worry on her face. There was a slight trembling of her hands. She was deeply troubled, that was certain, but of what was she so afraid?

Chad said softly, 'You must have taken something wrong, Candida. There's no reason for you to be upset. Glen Walker and I. . . .'

It was then that the door to the room burst in and Starr, looking a little the worse for wear after his night on the town, entered carrying his saddle. He looked at Candida with a smile on his lips. She rose from the chair and darted past him into the hallway.

'It seems that you had a night, too,' Starr said, dropping his saddle to the floor as he perched on his bed. Chad felt a little offended by the remark.

'She just came by a few minutes ago to discuss Glen Walker,' he said defensively.

'The same reason that I'm here,' Byron Starr

said, his smiling widening. He tipped his hat back. 'Walker drifted into the FitzRoy late last night and told me what had happened. He said you wanted me hired on as your deputy. For which I thank you, Chad. I can't believe it. Yesterday I hadn't a prospect. And now!'

'I guess they decided they didn't want Marshal Cody in office any longer.'

'Well, Chad, you've met the man. He didn't strike me as a whirlwind. Oh, well, out with the old, in with the new – that's the way everything goes in life, isn't it?'

'I suppose so,' Chad said glumly.

'Man, you should be grinning from ear to ear! What were your prospects when you came to Las Palmas?'

'Few and dim,' Chad answered.

'Well, cheer up, son! You know what else Walker told me last night? He's going to give us each an advance on our pay so we can buy some horses. Said he couldn't have his lawmen on foot.'

'*His* lawmen?'

'That's just a manner of speaking, Chad. This is no time to look these gift horses in the mouth. Not that I intend to. I saw a spry little sorrel at the stable that I wouldn't mind giving a try. We'll go back over there and see what else they have for sale.'

'I suppose that's an idea.'

'Sure it is! Then we find Glen Walker again and

make sure everything has been finalized with the mayor. Then we can go take a look at your new office and start figuring out this law business.'

Starr had taken a tin of saddle soap from his pack and was beginning to rub his leather with it to soften it up. He said, 'You should use some of this on your gunbelt and holster, Chad. They look like what they are – store-new and stiff.'

Both men made a pass at having breakfast which was *huevos rancheros* with freshly made buttered tortillas, but both were eager to get on with the new day. Chad had hoped to meet Candida at the table, but he was disappointed.

But as the two men tramped out of the door of the adobe and started toward town he turned his head once and saw a sad-eyed girl watching him from a window. He would have waved, but there was no point in it.

The sorrel Starr had admired was a fine, leggy four-year-old, which he took for a short ride before purchasing. Chad had practiced a speech to deliver to the one-eyed stable hand, but the man held up a hand.

'I heard all about it from Glen Walker earlier. 'You'll be wanting a horse, too, Marshal, is that right? Take your time looking around.'

'Did you hear what he called you?' Starr whispered as they walked the length of the stable and went out to survey the horses in the paddock beyond.

'Yes, I did,' Chad said. He ran an eye over the available stock in the horse pen, and yet a part of him was turned inward, wondering. He asked Starr, 'Doesn't this all seem a little sudden to you, Starr?'

'Yes, but this is a sudden place, a sudden time. Towns go up overnight; the next time you pass by they're only fit for packrats and ghosts. A dusty little town is withering away and the railroad decides to build a spur to it and suddenly you find a city there. Some old prospector who can't even feed himself happens upon the mother lode and the next time you see him, he's a millionaire in a dress suit. It's a sudden time, but I'm willing to catch a ride and take my chances with it. So should you be, Chad. Who knows when the next opportunity will present itself?'

After looking over the horses, Chad finally selected a heavy-footed buckskin. When he took it for a ride the animal moved eagerly, yet smoothly. If he were forced to do any long riding, this was the sort of horse he would want under him. 'I'll also need a saddle, the one he's wearing is fine – if that's all right with you,' he told the stable hand.

'It's fine by me. It's all profit, and Mr Walker said to give you boys what you needed.'

'I suppose the next thing is to get over to the marshal's office and take a look around – Walker might still be asleep. Do you want to just walk up the street?'

'Hell, no!' Starr answered. 'I've done enough walking lately to last me for some time. Let's take the ponies.'

So, riding the already active main street of Las Palmas, they swung down in front of the marshal's office and tied their new mounts loosely to the hitch rail.

'Here it is, son! Home,' Starr said loudly.

'I hope they didn't leave anyone behind in the cells,' Chad replied. Starr halted on the boardwalk, hands on his hips and looked steadily at Chad.

'If they did, we'll handle matters. You *are* the one for worrying about things that might never happen, aren't you?'

'I suppose,' Chad answered with a smile. 'Crack the door and let's see what kind of a mess they've left us.'

The door was open, so Starr swung it in. There was no key to the door; it had only a latch bar within to drop across it in times of trouble. The theory was that the office would never be deserted, and the prisoners would be in their cells anyway. The office was close, smelling of stale emptiness and sawdust. It took a minute to find the lantern on the wall. Starr had walked into the inner area of the jailhouse where the four cells stood, and returned to tell Chad, 'No one's locked up back there. What have you found?'

'Only these,' Chad said, pointing to the top of

the marshal's desk where a thick book of territorial law had been placed. On its cover the town marshal's badge rested.

'That's little help,' Starr said, glancing at the book as he seated himself in a wooden chair beside the desk. 'Better check out the drawers. There must be something on town ordinances in there – those will concern us more.'

'You're right,' Chad said. Opening the top drawer of the desk, he saw something shiny glinting there, He tossed it to Starr. 'Deputy's badge. You'd better get used to wearing it.'

'I notice you haven't pinned yours on yet, Marshal,' Starr said.

'I will in a minute.' He hefted Marshal Cody's badge and said thoughtfully, 'It's heavier than it looks.'

'You can handle it, Chad.' Starr was in the process of pinning his own badge on his blue-checked shirt.

'I hope so,' Chad said, awkwardly affixing the badge to the black shirt he wore on that morning. 'Is it straight?'

'Looks good to me,' Starr said. A shadow was cast across the patch of sunlight from the open door of the jail and both men looked that way. A man in his late twenties, looking haggard and half-drunk stood there, reeling in the sunlight. A patch of his shirt had been torn away from where a pocket should have been.

Starr rode lazily to his feet. 'What happened, son? Get into a fight, did you?'

'No, I didn't,' the stranger answered. He smelled sour, the expression on his face was sour. His hands were trembling. 'I'm Deacon Forge. I expect you know me.'

'I can't say that I do,' Starr answered calmly, squinting at the man in the sunlight.

Chad thought he knew the name. 'Deacon Forge, they call you "Deke", right?' At the man's nod, Chad told Starr, 'This is Marshal Cody's deputy.'

'I was until you two showed up,' Deke Forge said, panting as if he could not breathe in the musty room. 'Now I'm nothing!' His voice squeaked a little as he tried to shout that out. 'The fat man, Cody, he didn't say a word when they told him about it. Just put that book and his badge on the desk and walked away. What does he care? He's washed up anyway, and he's got a pension to live off of.

'Me! I've got no pension, only responsibilities. I owe money. I could work around that so long as I knew I had a steady paycheck coming to me every month. Now I've got just about enough coin to go get good and drunk on, and that's what I intend to do. I hope Glen Walker rots in hell with you two holding his hands. This was a low, underhanded move, even for him!'

Starr still appeared calm and Chad let him speak for them. 'Listen, Deacon, we're not going to have any trouble with you over this, are we?'

'Oh, yes,' Deke said tightly as he backed toward the door, 'you are going to have a lot of trouble with me. What snakes you are!'

Then he turned and stomped out of the office. Starr closed the heavy door behind him so that the room went dark again, only the lantern burning low to illuminate it. 'Come on, Chad,' Starr said with some heartiness. 'He's only a disgruntled employee, another man who's lost his job. I don't know, but it seems he might not have been much of a deputy anyway. Besides, men always talk that way to law officers – you'd better get used to it.'

'I suppose,' Chad said unhappily. He had a natural aversion to being disliked, but what was he to do about it? He had found the thin, well-thumbed folder containing the town ordinances with innumerable penciled notations by someone – Ben Cody, probably – in the margins. He would have to find the time to study it thoroughly. No matter what Starr, Glen Walker or anyone else thought of him, he intended to do this job as well as he could.

He tossed the folder onto the desk and turned to more practical matters. 'We're going to have someone on duty around the clock,' he told Starr. 'Unless we can find a way to authorize another deputy we'll have to work twelve-hour shifts. And since Cody was getting along with only one deputy, I think they'll expect us to continue like that.'

'You're right,' Starr agreed. 'I'd really prefer to be on nights anyway. Walking around, I saw a cot in the back storage room. I can sleep in there until I can find better accommodations in town.'

'If you wouldn't mind. . . .'

'I told you I prefer it,' Starr said, and Chad thought briefly of the tall red-headed girl Starr had met the night before in FitzRoy's. Yes, maybe he would prefer the night shift. 'I was just an uninvited guest in the aunts' house anyway. You stay there, Chad. It'll work out fine, you'll see.'

'We'll give it a try,' Chad agreed. 'If there's any problem, we can adjust later. For now, we'll work it that way.'

Chad surveyed the room with a sort of dawning pride. He had a steady, respectable job, a horse, a place to stay and a good friend. Or two. He wasn't about to forget that if it had not been for Glen Walker and Starr he would be begging for a job as a dish-washer or stable hand right now.

The door opened and Glen Walker himself entered the jail house, smiling.

He was wearing a dark suit with a ribbon tie, and smiling widely. 'Good morning, men. How's everything going? Are those your horses outside?'

'We were just working out a work schedule,' Chad

said. 'That is . . . is everything all settled now, officially?' There was still a little uneasiness in the back of his mind. Glen Walker brushed away his doubts.

'Oh, yes. Pettit talked to Mayor Swanson last night and the mayor gave his approval. The city council was all for replacing Marshal Cody with a younger man. You're it, Chad: our marshal. Any problems so far?'

'Only Deacon Forge,' Starr put in. He was perched on the corner of Chad's desk now, watching Walker.

'It was nothing,' Chad said hastily.

'He did the next thing to threatening us. I think that's something.'

'Pay no attention to Deke,' Glen Walker said. 'He's like that – a little volatile, but basically harmless. Was he drunk?'

'He was a little unsteady for this time of the morning,' Chad admitted.

'He was drunk,' Starr said flatly.

'All right, so he got himself some liquid courage and then came over here to complain. He's only a little man who got kicked off the gravy train. And he rode that long enough. He was useless as a law officer. If he shows up again, arrest him for being drunk. Otherwise, I wouldn't give him a thought. He's not worth it.'

Glen Walker went on. 'I see you've found Ben Cody's copy of the town ordinances.' He picked it up and thumbed through it curiously. 'Old Ben, he was just about useless, but he was a stickler for the law, I'll give him that much credit.

'The mayor and town council are just about finished working on an amended version of the codes. I'll see that you receive a copy of the new ordinances as soon as they are printed. Meanwhile, just try to keep our citizens from killing each other,' he added with another full smile.

Walker glanced at his watch, frowned, and started for the door once more. 'Excuse me, men. I've other business to attend to, and I don't want to keep you from your work.' He paused at the doorway and looked back at Chad. 'One thing you might want to keep an eye out for: Domino Jones is already back on his feet and roaming the town. I have to talk to Judge Lambert. I don't know if we could make an attempted murder charge stick or not, but he's bound to be carrying a grudge against you for the shooting, Chad.'

As Walker strode out of the room, Starr commented, 'Well, it looks like everything is in place for us. What do I do? Patrol the streets and show people my badge so that they know that something has changed in Las Palmas?'

'That seems all right,' Chad Dempster said. 'Look into the local saloons and make sure there's no trouble. But don't forget, Starr, Deacon Forge and Domino Jones are out there somewhere, wandering around.'

'I've seen Deacon Forge,' Starr said confidently. 'He's not a man to worry me. And Jones only has one good arm, and it's his gun arm he was shot in. I figure I can take care of myself with either of them.'

Confidence was fine, Chad thought as Starr sauntered toward the door and went out, but he was still worried, and he had none of Starr's confidence. He tilted back in the marshal's chair and stretched out a hand to pick up the folder containing the town ordinances. If he were going to enforce the law, he needed at least an understanding of what they were.

He spent an hour reading the book. By then the sun had shifted so that it glowed brightly into the room and Chad rose to shut the shades. Before he could take his chair again, his first small bit of humiliation came his way.

A buckboard drawn by two scrawny-looking horses drew up in front of his office and a man with a straw hat swung down, handing the reins to a woman in a white bonnet. Three kids of various ages fooled around in the bed of the wagon. The man stamped up to the office door, swung it open and came in, removing his hat as he saw Chad.

' 'Morning, Marshal. Where can I find the courthouse?'

'I'm not sure,' Chad stammered. The man eyed him coldly as if a cruel prank were being played on him.

'You're the marshal here and you don't know where the courthouse is?'

Chad brazened it out. 'Just up the street.'

'Which side?' the man demanded.

'You'll find it,' Chad answered. And he was sure the man would, but not from his directions. The man frowned, placed his hat on his balding head deliberately and turned to stalk out again. Chad could hear him saying something angrily to the woman.

After they pulled off, Chad was given time to reflect. He hadn't met the mayor of the town, didn't know the local judge by sight – only his name, Lambert. Did not know where the courthouse was, nor the city hall, if there was one. Placing the town ordinances aside for a while, he picked up his hat, deciding that he should take a little tour to familiarize himself with Las Palmas. So far he knew only two streets and one alley, hardly enough should trouble begin somewhere and he was asked for help. Tomorrow, he decided, he would take his new horse, ride the outlying area and mentally map it, looking at the local ranches and small farms and, if possible, finding out the names of the residents.

For today, he figured it would be enough to learn where the courthouse stood and trying to memorize the patterns of the local streets and their names, if they bore any, so that if he was called to respond to trouble, he would have an idea of where he was going.

After a few hours of mostly aimless riding in the heat of the day he returned to the office to find that Starr had returned.

'I thought that maybe something had happened to you,' Starr said, rising from behind Chad's desk.

'No. I just thought I should have a look around town.'

'I spent my time around the saloons,' Starr told him. 'I walked up on a couple of fistfights. One of them broke up when they saw my badge. At the other I had to crack a man over the skull with my pistol. It seemed easier than dragging them back over to the jail and trying to figure out what happened.'

'I suppose that was all right,' Chad said hesitantly. 'We'll have to set some kind of policy for future problems. At least they know the law is alive and well in Las Palmas.'

'What I was wondering,' Starr asked through a yawn, 'is when the law is going to be on the alert in this town. What I mean, Chad, is that we agreed we were going to try to work twelve on and twelve hours off and see how it worked. If I'm going to start tonight, when do I begin? I didn't get a lot of sleep last night, and I could use a nap.'

Chad thought for a minute and answered, 'Let's try having you take eight at night until eight o'clock in the morning as your shift.' He shrugged. 'All of this is trial and error, Starr. We can always change it.

Can you live with that for now?'

Starr seemed unconcerned. 'We'll give it a shot. I'll try out that cot in the storeroom and see if it fits me. Wake me up before you leave.'

'All right. Starr, if anyone should ask you, the courthouse is on Main Street just past Fletcher. South side of the road.'

SIX

'So it seems you are terrible smart, after all,' Carmalita said as she bounded onto the hotel room bed where Glen Walker sat cleaning his Colt. She was like an eager puppy dog, her eyes bright. 'You have everything in your plan working.'

Walker was feeling patient. He placed his pistol on the bedside table and nodded, taking Carmalita by the arms. 'All that's left is to have the new town laws approved by the council, and Mayor Swanson is going to ram that through, explaining the need to pay for improved law enforcement in Las Palmas, and at least hinting that the new assessment on businesses will also mean a boost in the council's pay.'

'Five per cent of every dollar spent in this town will be ours,' Carmalita said with a contended sigh, rolling over onto her back to look up at Glen Walker. 'And you will build me the finest house in Las Palmas – in the territory!'

'That's what I promised, what I always told you would happen if you stuck with me.'

Carmalita propped herself up on one elbow, her dark hair draping her eyes. 'That is what I told my cousin, Candida, when we went over to the adobe last night. I told her you are a man to keep your promises.'

'What do you mean?' Glen Walker asked sharply. 'How much of my plan did you tell her?'

Fear crept across Carmalita's eyes. 'Only that much . . . what difference can it make now, Glen? I was only bragging to her about you.'

'I don't know if it can make any difference,' Walker replied. Still he was uneasy about anyone outside of the inner circle knowing that it was he, Glenn Walker, who was the man behind the scenes, orchestrating the looting of Las Palmas. The business owners would be angry when they found out that they were going to be taxed an extra five per cent of their incomes in order to have the town provide law enforcement for the town, but that would die down. They might vote the mayor out of office, turn on the town council, but by then the law would already be on the books and it would take years of legal wrangling to get it changed – if it could ever be changed. In the meantime Walker meant to enjoy the profits of the scheme without having to take a share of the blame.

The merchants would not be happy with

Tanglefoot if he were needed to enforce the new tax, but that was just too bad for the kid.

'Maybe I'd be better off working with Starr,' Glen Walker said.

'Who is Starr?'

'You know – Chad Dempster's deputy. He seems a more worldly man, and I think he has sand in his craw.'

'Sand. . . ?' Carmalita said, unfamiliar with the expression.

'A tougher man. Starr has ridden a few rough trails somewhere along the line, I'll guarantee you. Skinny Jim told me that it was Starr who shot down a couple of Domino Jones's men at Lone Pine. I suspect it was also Starr who shot Domino and killed Charlie Burnett in town. I wonder what Joe Meyer, the blacksmith, saw happen? I'll have to remember to ask him.'

Carmalita was yawning on the bed. The day was creeping up toward noon and it was time for her siesta. 'If you want this Starr instead, why don't you just tell them,' she asked.

Why don't I? Walker was wondering. But it wouldn't be that easy. He had spent a lot of time and effort building up Dempster as an honest man and a hero fit to replace old Ben Cody, which idea had appealed to Mayor Swanson, Judge Lambert and the town council. He couldn't just suddenly shift his preference for town marshal to Starr, could he?

But it was something to ponder. He intended to talk to Starr and to give it a lot of thought. In the meantime he meant to find out a little more about this Byron Starr's background.

When Chad had roused the deep-sleeping Starr and started on his way home aboard the stolid buckskin horse it was a quarter past eight, and the saloons along Main Street, FitzRoy's, the Silver Eagle and the Clipper were already going great guns, doing a loud, lusty business. Well – that was Starr's business: keeping a lid on the festivities for the night, and he had little doubt that Starr was up to it.

There was a weirdly lighted sunset sky to the west. Thin clouds had formed themselves into diffused streamers against the red background, the dying sun shining through them wove long filaments of gold, resembling the crazy patterns of black widow-spider webs. Chad looked that way for a long while as the world around him went darker. As he was passing a stand of four large oak trees, black against the sundown sky, a shot rang out near at hand. The bullet missed him, but whipped by near enough for him to hear. The report followed – a Colt .44.

Chad slapped at his own pistol riding in its new holster and had fumbled it out before a second shot was fired in his direction. He went to the side of his horse and flagged the buckskin toward home. He had been watching the shadows in town, but once clear of Las Palmas, he had let his attention waver. No matter, he could have not out-shot the man in the trees. He was fortunate the man was unsteady – drunk? – enough to miss.

It was not Domino Jones who had ambushed him. That was not Jones's style, anyway. Chad had gotten only a glimpse of the gunman, but thought he seemed familiar. In build he resembled Deacon Forge, one of the few men in town who had a grudge against Chad Dempster. His quick impression of the man was certainly not enough to arrest Forge.

Riding on, Chad glanced at the pistol he still held in his hand, then he shoved it back into its holster. This could not continue – he would have to make the time to go off and practice with his handgun, at least enough to achieve a small degree of proficiency.

He would find the time; he must.

There was that, and studying the town ordinances, of which he had only the thinnest knowledge so far. He wondered idly if old Ben Cody would be willing to help him. But the man, if not embittered, had nothing to profit by tutoring his sudden replacement. Chad would have to manage on his own.

Then there was familiarizing himself with surrounding country. He needed to know who the landowners were there, as well as in town. It was a lot to try to absorb in a few days. Ben Cody had years of experience with everyone in the town and its environs. It was too bad that the transfer of authority had not taken place in a more measured way. The old man must know much that he could have taught to Chad.

Why had he even taken the job, Chad wondered? Partly out of loyalty to Glen Walker, certainly, and because with no other prospects – as Starr had reminded him – they could have found themselves now out on the desert, living off rattlesnake meat.

Chad could not shake the gloom he felt. With the adobe house now in sight, he slowed the buckskin horse rather than riding up to it in triumph. He had been shot at, overwhelmed with doubts about his own capabilities, and was carrying heavy misgivings. He had much to do, and little time to accomplish it.

Under these circumstances he should have felt annoyed at what he discovered waiting for him when he arrived at the adobe, but Candida's appearance on the front porch gladdened his heart and made the other concerns of his day seem irrelevant.

Her mood, however, was not cheerful as he swung down from the buckskin, hitched it and stepped up onto the porch. She still wore her pink dress; her eyes were still wide, uncertain.

'Did you have a good day?' she asked. 'Did the job. . . ?'

'Everything went all right,' he said, stepping toward her, which caused her to back away. Frowning, she said:

'I ask because we thought we heard some gunfire from down the road.'

'It wasn't me,' Chad said, trying to defuse the girl's anxiety. Just why should it cause her to worry?

'I am glad,' Candida said with a calmness that was fabricated. 'It won't be the end of it, Chad,' she said in a rush of words, 'It is only the beginning. You should not stay in this town. You should travel far and fast. You have a horse now, I see . . . go before they trap you into their web of deceit and fraud.'

He couldn't understand her. *What was the woman talking about?*

'Does this have something to do with what your cousin told you last night?' he asked.

'Yes.' She took the fabric of the arms of both sleeves of his shirt in her hands, stepped forward and stared up with star-bright eyes. 'You do not see it.' She struggled to find the right English words and told him most solemnly, 'You are their sacrificial lamb, Chad Dempster.'

As Chad struggled to find a response to this odd statement, the front door of the adobe swung open wide and Aunt Margarita appeared in the doorway. With a firm voice, but understanding smile, she told Candida,

'A young girl should not be left alone in the

moonlight with a young man for too long, Candida.'

'No, Tia Margarita,' Candida answered.

After the door had closed, leaving them alone in the darkness, Candida said, 'I must talk to you, Chad. About what I had mentioned.'

'Yes, about Glen Walker? You need to make that clear.'

'It is my cousin who told me – she and Walker are very close.'

'I know that. When can we talk? Tonight, in my room?'

Candida laughed. 'No, I am afraid not! If my aunt doesn't like me standing out here with you for so long, she will certainly notice if I were to dare to come to your room.'

'I suppose you're right. You could try coming by the marshal's office tomorrow.'

'No, not there! Then everyone would know that I had business with you. It would get back to Glen Walker.'

'I don't know, then,' Chad said. 'I have to be back at the office by eight o'clock to relieve Starr. If you rise earlier than that, I can meet you in the canyon beyond the pasture – I have business there.'

'In the canyon?' Candida asked curiously.

'Yes, there is something I must do there. Every morning, I think. Come there if you can get away from the house.'

Candida nodded, shrugged her thin shoulders and bit gently at her lower lip. She turned to start toward the door, but took the time to add, 'I think you are a strange man, Charles Dempster.'

'Yes, I'm beginning to think that myself,' he replied.

Candida slipped into the well-lighted house then. Beyond her Chad could see both of the guardian aunts watching her with folded arms. He gave them time to clear the room by stabling his horse before he opened the door again and went in, striding toward his bed. Aunt Rosa stopped him, a worried look on her round face.

'Don't you wish to eat tonight, Señor Dempster? I have fresh-made *enchiladas* in the oven.'

'Not tonight,' Chad told the obviously disappointed woman. He touched her shoulder. 'Thank you for being concerned about me.'

'Oh, yes,' she said, looking directly into his eyes. 'I am concerned for you in many ways.' Then she turned and walked away toward the kitchen.

What was going on around here? Everything was going well for Chad, but everyone had fear that he was in over his head. Well, maybe he was. He knew that he had at least two armed enemies out there – Domino Jones and Deacon Forge. He knew he had no experience as a law officer, but had been given an entire town to watch over, a town he knew nothing about. He tossed his hat aside and sat on his bed, wishing he were more like Byron Starr, who was undoubtedly keeping his watch on the town from a table at FitzRoy's where the leggy redhead – what was her name? Peggy? – worked. So long as it was done, it probably made no difference, at least the residents of Las Palmas knew that the law was still being maintained there.

After kicking his boots off, Chad lay on his back, removing his copy of the town ordinances from his shirt where he had tucked it. By lantern light, he read until he could not keep his eyes open any longer.

One paragraph caught his eye because Ben Cody had scrawled numerous notes and exclamation marks beside it. Most of the pencil-scrawled notes were indecipherable and there was a lot of profanity included in them. The paragraph read:

Section 2, Point 7: The right of landholders and every tax-paying citizen to free law-enforcement protection under the constitution of this town is hereby guaranteed, the cost of such law-enforcement to be liened against said property taxes.

It was an awkward sentence, written by legal minds which seldom dabble in plain English, but Chad took it to mean, if you lived in Las Palmas and paid your taxes, you got law enforcement paid for by your taxes. That seemed plain enough. Why then had Marshal Cody been concerned enough or angry enough to scribble profanity-laced notes all over the borders of the ordinance book? It was one more item he thought he should talk to Cody about – if the man would agree to see him.

When he could not keep his eyes propped open any longer, Chad turned the lantern down, undressed and climbed into bed. He tried to sort through his problems, real and imagined, for a while as he turned and twisted on the bed, but he had little luck. His thoughts kept returning to the wide-eyed woman with the easy smile, and at last he fell to sleep, still thinking of Candida.

There was the faintest glimmer of light through the bedroom window when a distantly barking dog brought Chad awake. The barking should have annoyed him, but he had been eager to start the new day early.

Yawning, he rose. No one else could be heard stirring in the house. Chad dressed and snatched up a box of .44 cartridges that Starr had left behind – he could be paid back later. How were the office supplies, Chad wondered inconsequentially, and who should he see to ask for funds if needed? He shook his head and wondered again at a man who would take a job about which he knew so little.

He managed to slip out of the house without waking anyone. In the dawn light he walked toward the canyon beyond the pasture. He could see the crowns of the cottonwood trees – called alamosa in the Southwest – and picked his way over the broken ground toward them. A single, somewhat belliger-ent white goat made a few nervous rushes toward him, but they were only for show.

Finding a spot in the shade of the cottonwood trees, he checked his weapon and eyed a few possi-ble targets on the sandy bank. He was determined to get better at shooting, no matter how late he was in trying to acquire the skill. Speed and accuracy – he wanted to learn both, although an old man down on the Kansas line had told him once, 'There's those with speed and those with accuracy. All I can say is that those with accuracy are the ones who are mostly still alive.'

It was good advice, Chad thought, but he had seen the slick, easy draw of Byron Starr, seen the accuracy of his shooting. He might never be that good, but he meant to try. His first attempt at a quick draw opened his eyes to the reality of matters. He very nearly shot himself in the foot, having drawn back the hammer too soon. When was the proper instant to do that? Maybe Starr could give him some pointers.

It was not warm, but perspiration was in Chad's eyes after he had banged off twenty or thirty rounds, missing his target almost every time. He hadn't expected to become instantly expert in this, but it was frustrating. He had fired at a hand-sized chalky rock on the bank of the canyon dozens of time, and not even creased it. Still, he thought he was getting smoother with his draw. Maybe that was all a man could expect on his first day.

Reloading, he noticed that he was no longer alone in the canyon.

She wore blue jeans and a red-checked shirt – unusual garb for a Spanish woman. Where she had come from, Chad could not say, but she had slipped up behind him to stand behind the trunk of one of the old cottonwood trees, from where she had been watching. He studied her, feeling foolish.

'If that rock was Glen Walker, you would be dead, Charles Dempster.'

'Is he good with a gun? I've never seen him shoot.'

'He is the best, my cousin says.' She shrugged, 'But then Carmalita thinks he is the best at every-thing.'

'I guess this must look silly to you,' Chad said as he reloaded his pistol again.

'What? Trying to learn how to survive?' She shook her head. 'No, I think it is only wise.'

'But not as wise as running away would be?'

'Ah, you are a man – I knew I could not persuade you to run away from trouble,' she said with a little shake of her head. 'So this is the next best thing for you to do, I think.'

'I've a long way to go,' Chad said, looking down at his revolver as he snapped its loading gate shut.

'Yes, I think so as well,' Candida said frankly, 'but you are trying, as you are trying to learn a new and difficult job. Even if they do not really want you to learn it.'

'What do you mean?' he asked testily. 'Of course they do. They want strong law enforcement in Las Palmas. Does this have something to do with that "sacrificial lamb" business you mentioned?'

'It does, according to Carmalita,' she answered softly, leaning her back against the trunk of the tree.

'And how would she know?' Chad growled.

'Because she is closest to the ring-man. How do you say it?'

'The ringleader?' Chad suggested.

'Yes, that is it.' She had one leg drawn up behind her as she tilted her body back against the tree. 'Glen Walker is that man, the ringleader.'

'I don't understand you,' he said impatiently as angrily he thrust his pistol into its holster. 'You must have misunderstood something you heard.'

'No, my cousin and I both speak very good Spanish. Carmalita has told me all. You are a victim here, Chad Dempster, and when they are through with you they will kill you.'

SEVEN

It wasn't easy to find the small clapboard house, and it was still early in the day, an unlikely time for an unwelcome visit, but Chad had left Starr snoring on his office cot and ridden to Ben Cody's house. It was time they spoke. The old lawman likely knew more of what was going on around Las Palmas than anyone.

Chad felt that there was much more he had to learn. He was lost, adrift in things he did not understand. If Cody would deign to speak with him, perhaps much could be cleared up. He owed it to the town, to himself, to Candida who had urged him to dig deeper into matters in Las Palmas. Hell, he owed it to the citizenry he was now sworn to protect.

There was a cottonwood tree standing in front of Ben Cody's modest house, and a buggy with its traces dropped near a hitch rail. The buggy did not surprise Chad. What would have been more surprising would be the sight of the corpulent former marshal sitting a saddle horse. After tying his horse to the hitching rail with a loose slip knot, Chad stepped uneasily up onto the shadowy porch of the small cottage. If Cody had reason to dislike anyone in town, Chad's name was certainly at the top of the list. He rapped twice on the door and waited, expecting anything.

The door was swung wide suddenly and Ben Cody stood there, wearing an apron, a wooden spoon in his hand. The former marshal smiled.

'Come in, young man! I was just making breakfast. If I have to say it myself, I've gotten to be a fair cook since my wife passed away three years ago. Can I offer you anything?'

Chad was taken aback by the former marshal's joviality. 'No,' he stammered, 'though if that's fresh coffee I smell. . . .'

'It is. I just ground the beans this morning. It'll be ready before you can sit and make yourself comfortable – Dempster? That's right, isn't it?'

'That's right.' Chad said, holding his hat in his hand, looking around the small comfortable-appearing room.

'I've scrambled some eggs,' Cody said. 'Eight of them, though I usually only eat six. You've never had them the way I fix them – a little cream, a few diced onions, a tomato and just a tablespoon of

90

brown sugar. I wish I could talk you into trying some.'

'Well, maybe I will,' Chad said, since he had been on the road before the aunts were up and about.

Cody stirred the eggs cooking in the black skillet on the stove, then poured them each a cup of coffee. 'Cook them slow,' Ben Cody said, 'that's the trick to it. Now then,' he asked, putting his heavy forearms on the table and looking across at Chad, 'what brings you out here so early in the morning?'

On this day, the old man with the round face and the small nose seemed almost cherubic, far from Chad's first impression of him. He rose again to check his eggs. 'Go ahead and eat,' Chad said. 'We can talk around it.'

Cody scraped the contents of his skillet onto a plate and brought it steaming to the table. The mound of eggs on Cody's platter seemed almost enough for two men, but then, Chad reflected, the bulky ex-marshal was nearly the size of two men.

Chad began hesitantly. 'I was wondering about a few things. For instance, I've been reading the county ordinances and something I saw in there worried me.'

'Section two, point seven?' Cody asked, his mouth full of scrambled eggs. 'You know, I have to admit my wife did a better job with this than I do.' He pointed at his platter. 'It takes some time to learn every skill, I expect.'

91

'Maybe she put butter in it,' Chad said for something to say before returning to his main point.

'You know – that may be it. You might be right, Dempster. I'll try it next time.'

'Marshal Cody, why did you immediately think I was talking about Section two, point seven. It drew my eye at first only because of all your pencilled remarks. But why that one sentence?'

'Because, son,' Cody said, pushing away his plate and leaning back to stretch, 'that's where all your trouble lies. It's why I was fired and you were hired.'

'I don't understand you,' Chad was forced to admit. The marshal rose and put his dishes in the sink. When he turned back again, his eyes were much more serious.

'I was hoping that you didn't,' Cody said. 'Because if you did . . .' He paused and seated himself, starting again. 'It's plain theft that they're planning. A clerk I know in the courthouse showed me a copy of the revised town statutes last week. They have amended it to say that every landowner and businessman in Las Palmas must now pay a five per cent surtax if he wants protection from the town marshal's office.'

'But that's. . . !'

'Taxation by decree. And if you'll remember your history it's one of the reasons this country chose to break free of England. But once that is on the books, it'll be the law whether people like it or not.'

'Will people pay it?'

'Let's just say there will be some reluctance. To put it mildly,' the former marshal said with a faint smile. 'After all, no one voted on this, no one was told in advance. Yes, there will be some reluctance.'

'What will the mayor, the town, do?'

'Well, they'll have to send someone to collect the money, won't they? I told them flat out that I would have no part of it, and so they found themselves a new man to become a bill collector – that's you, my young friend. They'll have you out intimidating people in town, or trying to. Which is not my idea of law enforcement, and is why you find me sitting contentedly at home in my own kitchen with a full belly.'

Chad was silent for a long minute. Beyond the house a cow lowed. The sun, seen through the kitchen window, rose higher. 'I'll have to quit,' Chad said suddenly. His hands were clenched tightly.

'Can you?' Cody asked. 'These people have put you in their debt, and you know it. You've taken their money, haven't you?'

'A little,' Chad said numbly.

'They'll try to convince you that you should take more. They want you as a hired thug. One who wears a badge and has the law behind him, but a thug all the same.' Cody looked wistfully at the badge Chad was wearing, as if he had worn it proudly and was about to see it shamed. Cody rose, turning his eyes away.

'One more thing, Mr Dempster – if you think that walking into the town's saloons and trying to collect the tax is going to be hell, wait until you try dealing with the cattlemen on the outlying ranches. There are some hard men riding the range.'

'I can imagine. If I had any money I'd hop back on the stage and ride it out of town.'

'They'd only find someone else for the job,' Cody told him.

'I suppose, but it would no longer be my problem.'

'I think,' Cody said, eyeing him closely, 'it will always be your problem until it's solved one way or the other. Drop around and see me sometime. I'll make another stab at scrambling eggs – it's about all I know how to cook.'

Cody walked Chad to the front door and saw him mount his horse. When the fat former marshal closed the door, Chad was still just sitting there, though the horse beneath him shuddered impatiently, wanting to move.

So that was what Candida had been trying to tell him. Her cousin, presumably wishing to brag about Glen Walker's cleverness, had revealed the plan in some detail, whether she had intended to or not. A sacrificial lamb was what Candida had said. It was too true – if he were sent out to enforce the new tax law, he would have to face some angry armed men. Candida had told him to just hit the trail, ride away from Las Palmas and its problems, and perhaps she was right. But, as Cody had told him, they would just find someone else to take his place and nothing would have been done to solve the political looting of the town.

There had to be a third way, but what?

Glen Walker was wearing an ivory-colored suit and a scarlet cravat this morning as he crossed the street, heading to the marshal's office from his hotel room. He did not see the buckskin horse that Chad Dempster had been riding tied in front of the office, only Byron Starr's leggy sorrel. Was Dempster late to work on his second day? It did not matter; things would be easier this way.

Walker found Byron Starr standing next to the iron stove in the office, sipping a cup of coffee. He also thought he could smell whiskey on the deputy. That, too, was of no importance to Walker.

'Did you have a busy night?' Glen Walker asked as he took the marshal's chair behind the scarred desk.

'Not bad,' Starr answered. 'One fist fight in the Clipper, a man waving a gun around in the FitzRoy. I didn't bother to arrest anyone, just told them to take it somewhere else.'

'You seem to have things under control,' Walker

said, measuring the deputy with the curly hair and cold blue eyes.

'I'm trying.'

'Where's our marshal this morning?'

'I haven't seen him yet. He might have dropped in while I was asleep.'

Walker nodded and stroked his cleanly shaven chin. Without further hesitation, he asked Starr, 'How would you like to make an extra hundred a month?'

Starr's eyes narrowed, whether with suspicion or avarice was difficult for Glen Walker to determine.

'I don't get you, Walker. If it's anything illegal, you have the wrong man.'

'Not that you haven't ever done anything dirty in your time – I've checked up on you, Starr.'

'Well, when I was younger and even dumber, I got caught up in a few small things. . . .'

'Is that what they call a string of bank hold-ups these days?'

'That was a long time ago,' Starr said, thumping his empty tin cup down on the stove.

'Not so very long ago,' Walker said smoothly. 'There may still be warrants out on whoever participated in those robberies. I haven't found that out yet.'

'I'm not going back to anything illegal,' Starr said, sitting on the corner of the desk to face Glen Walker.

'I'm not asking you to,' Walker replied in that silky tone he always used when he needed to sway someone. 'Just the opposite, as a matter of fact. I'm asking you to enforce a new law the mayor and the council just enacted. I haven't talked to Dempster yet. Frankly I don't think he has the kind of experience this job will take. Let me show you what I'm talking about.'

From the inside pocket of his suit coat, Glen Walker removed a newly printed copy of the relevant ordinance. He passed it to Starr and watched as the deputy scanned it.

'You want me to enforce this?' is what Starr said after folding it and handing it back. 'The public won't stand for it.'

'They'll stand for it because they'll have to.' Walker shrugged. 'If they don't pay the assessed tax, they'll be thrown in jail – by you. When they go to court, Judge Lambert will tell them that they have to pay or go right back to jail – if not the territorial prison.'

Starr was concerned; he rubbed his tired eyes and asked, 'What does Chad Dempster have to say about this?'

'Old Tanglefoot?' Walker laughed out loud. 'Nothing, because I haven't talked to him about it. He's not our man, Starr, you are – for an extra hundred dollars a month.'

'I'd be risking my life trying to collect this tax.'

'And what do you think you're doing every night, just wearing that badge? At least this way, it profits you.'

Starr was visibly upset. 'Can I think this over?'

'Of course,' Walker said, 'but you know that if you refuse to perform your duties as a lawman, you will be discharged.'

Starr nodded. The pressure Walker was exerting was twofold. One, he needed the money, two, Walker somehow knew about Starr's involvement in the bank robberies down south. Starr had almost believed that the law had forgotten about him, or at least had lost interest in him, and that he was starting a new, upright life in Las Palmas. Some things in the past just can't be left behind. They ride with you like haunting ghosts.

'I'll think things over,' Starr said again.

'Sure.' Hat adjusted on his barbered hair, Walker nodded and made his way toward the door of the jailhouse. 'Don't take too long,' he added, 'I'm going to stop in at FitzRoy's. Is there anything you'd like me to tell Peggy?'

Starr just shook his head. Walker smiled and went out. Had that been some sort of veiled threat? And how did Walker even know about Peggy Kimball? Of course, the man seemed to know everything that went on in Las Palmas. Starr certainly hadn't tried to keep it a secret. He sat down in the marshal's wooden chair and considered his immediate future.

He could go along with Walker on his strictly legal plan to shake down the local businessmen and find himself wealthier for it. Or he could refuse Walker, in which case Starr's whereabouts might very well be given to the county sheriff. He could straddle his horse and ride out, deserting Las Palmas, Peggy Kimball and Chad Dempster until another horse died under him.

Starr glanced at the brass-bound clock on the wall and made his way back toward the cot where he was sleeping until he could afford a pleasant room that he could share with Peggy, hoping for a dreamless interval in his abruptly confusing life.

Starr was still asleep when Chad looped his reins over the hitch rail in front of the jailhouse and entered his office. He checked for prisoners and found there was none. Good. Starr was either doing his job quietly or the town had calmed down.

Unless Starr was not trying to do his job at all, but was using his nights to frequent the FitzRoy and spark that red-headed girl with the long legs. Somehow Chad did not believe that this was so; Starr had been happy to get this job, and seemed eager to make a success of it.

There was no one in the office, no notes on his desk, so Chad decided the best use he could make of the rest of the morning was to carry out his rounds on the street, letting people know he was still the law in Las Palmas.

It was a peaceful morning; the high sun was bright but not as hot as it had been lately. He came upon a boy trying to climb in the candy-shop window and, later, two drunks in the alley beside the Clipper, fighting on hands and knees like a pair of dogs. He chased all of them home. Starr was right about that – if they arrested everyone for small crimes they would soon run out of jail cells and Judge Lambert might resent having his calendar clotted up with these sorts of misdemeanors.

For the most part Las Palmas was quiet on this morning, leaving Chad with time – too much time – to think. Why had he thought that Glen Walker was a friend, helping him out as he had? He had only done it because he was planning to put a dupe into the marshal's office, one who would be obliged to Walker. An honest and brave man to replace the fading Ben Cody – who was probably the only honest man in town. Too honest to run this scam that Judge Lambert and Mayor Swanson had concocted, in cahoots with Walker along with the town councilmen, each of whom must be counting on receiving his cut of the tax money.

'What a fool I am,' Chad was thinking. Walker had put him up in a house that he owned, found him a meaningless job taking the Sunday stage east to Diablo when the regular driver and shotgun rider could have done it the day afterward.

The hold-up had been a sham. There were rifle-men posted near the lone pine to ambush the ambushers. That little bit of show had been per-formed only to convince people that Chad was the man for the job of marshal. A real gunslinger! Chad almost laughed out loud as he patrolled the back alleys of the town, finding nothing more unlawful than a pair of dogs digging through the Abbey Restaurant's garbage.

So, he had been a fool. How did he get out of this? If he tried to do what was right, he was dead in this town. How could he refuse to enforce the hastily enacted town ordinance no matter how much it reeked of local corruption? He couldn't, was the answer.

As Cody had reminded him, Walker and his mob could replace him easily if he let them down.

Chad hadn't calculated it, as Walker undoubtedly had, but he knew there was a lot of money involved, too much to let a recalcitrant lawman stand in the way of collecting it. Five per cent of the goods and services provided daily, even in a town this size, would add up rapidly.

No, Chad decided suddenly, he wanted no part of this, no part of Las Palmas, although he had been gradually becoming fond of the little desert com-munity.

Candida. The sudden thought of her caused him to stop in mid-stride as he circled back toward the jailhouse. She had urged him to go, but did she really wish for him to leave? Not that she would be left in a bad position. Her cousin, Carmalita, was destined to become quite a wealthy woman, married to an important man. The aunts would certainly take good care of Candida. What did she need Charles Dempster for, anyway?

But he thought he had once or twice seen the kind of longing in her eyes that he felt for her. Maybe it had been only concern for his safety. But if there was a chance. . . ?

As of the moment he was an appointed town official with a well-paying job which would be increased greatly if he only did his duty and enforced the new law. He would not be loved in town, but he would still be respected.

And if he just forked that buckskin horse and trailed out onto the desert, could Candida ever respect him? Could he respect himself?

You had to give it to Glen Walker – he knew how to throw his loop around a man.

EIGHT

Starr was up and out of bed when Chad reached the jail again. Drinking coffee, which smelled as if it were laced with something, Starr lifted his blood-shot blue eyes as Chad entered. His smile of welcome was easy; his words were abrupt.

'We have to talk, Chad.'

'What's happened?' Chad asked, noting the urgency in Starr's voice. He hung his gunbelt on one of the row of pegs provided, and sat behind his desk.

'Glen Walker came by,' Byron Starr said. His grip seemed a little unsteady on the tin cup he held.

'Oh? What did he want?'

'The way he was talking, he wants you out and me in as marshal.'

'Does he? Why do you think that is?'

'He seems to think that you're not able and willing to enforce this new ordinance they've cooked up.'

Chad was thoughtful for a moment. 'No,' he told Starr, 'I don't think I am.'

'The thing is, Chad,' Starr said dourly, 'I don't believe that I am either. It's a pure shakedown, charging people for something that their property taxes are already supposed to provide.'

'That's government for you,' Chad said. 'If they could figure out how to do it, they'd charge us for the air we breathe.'

'Well, I don't have to be a part of it,' Starr said. He was growing angry. He took another sip of whatever was in his cup and shook his head. 'The thing is, Chad – Walker has found a way of using leverage on me.'

'He's good at that,' Chad replied. 'Let's have it, Starr, what's he threatening you with?'

'I have . . . a bit of a background, Chad,' Starr replied. 'Somehow Walker has found out about it. It puts me in a bad position. He's holding that over my head.'

'What was it, Starr?' Chad asked, seriously interested.

'Bank robbery. Just a stupid impulse.' Starr sighed and drank some more of his coffee.

'Was anyone hurt?'

'No. But they still don't take kindly to bank robbery. I felt real bad about it. Once I sobered up I realized I was still as broke as ever and could not go home again. That's why I was so happy to get this job. I had determined to straighten out, and somehow make amends for my foolishness.'

'I can understand that,' Chad said. He thought that Starr was sincere. 'Are there warrants out on you still?'

'I didn't think so; Walker does. He's promised to look into it, which he can easily. If I leave now, he'll probably have Wanted posters printed on me, down to a description of the horse I'm riding.'

'It would put a lot of pressure on a man, knowing that might happen,' Chad said.

'If I stay here and do what they want it'll put me opposite the direction I was trying to go, Chad. It'll put me in with a gang of thieves again. And who knows if Walker would ever let me off the hook now that he has that power over me.'

'It's hell, isn't it? Him making you pay for trying to go straight.'

Starr had walked to the iron stove and poured himself another half-cup of coffee. When he had seated himself again in the chair behind the desk, he lifted those blurred eyes and said, 'Walker's gone to talk to Peggy Kimball at FitzRoy's.'

'Why would he do that?' Chad asked in amazement.

'If I had to guess,' Starr answered, 'I'd say he's going to tell her that they had decided to make me marshal – and at a hundred dollars more a month. That would be sure to make her happy. I'd be making enough to take her out of the saloon, find a little house for us. Then what do I do, Chad? Go over and tell her I'm just going to quit and make a run for the desert? It would crush the girl and make me out to be the lowest scoundrel she's ever met.'

Chad thought for a minute. 'I think you're probably right. It's the sort of maneuver Glen Walker would pull if he thought he needed to keep the pressure on you.'

Starr said fiercely, 'I ought to just shoot the man and have done with it.'

'You know that wouldn't solve anything,' Chad said lightly. 'Then I'd just have to try to arrest you and bring you in here. Judge Lambert would be sure to sentence you to hang. Peggy's hopes would still be crushed – and someone else would still be out collecting taxes.'

'Deacon Forge most likely. Say, Chad, have you seen him around anywhere?'

'No,' Chad had to tell him. Which was odd, since they knew that Forge frequented the gambling tables at the Clipper saloon. 'It could be that he owes some people too much money to risk showing his face in town. He as much as told us that.' Chad hesitated and added: 'Although I might have seen him yesterday – I just couldn't be sure.' Starr's eyebrows lifted questioningly. 'Someone took a shot at me on my way back to the adobe,' Chad told him.

'Maybe it was Domino Jones,' Starr said. 'I

haven't seen that brute around town either.' Starr exhaled heavily. 'Either one of them wouldn't mind gunning both of us down.'

'I guess not,' Chad answered. 'We sure have managed to get ourselves in a fix, Starr. And it didn't take us much time at all.'

'No. The question is, Chad: is there any way out of it for us?'

Chad continued to ponder Starr's question as the weary deputy again staggered off to sleep on his cot for a few hours before eight o'clock rolled around. A wise man once said that there was always a way. Or maybe the man was a fool. Chad could not see a path out. He wished he had a more intimate knowledge of the town's inner workings. Of course he had not – that was precisely why he had been hired. He thought that he wouldn't mind talking to Ben Cody again.

That was because he had the faintest glimmering of a thought. Nothing firm, but a vague idea of how he and Starr might get out of this fix alive. He put his boots up on the desk and leaned back in Cody's chair. And pondered.

And pondered.

It was too soon to mention his idea to Starr, so the tortured deputy would just have to wade through his present dismal feeling for a while longer. The sun heeled over and slowly sank. The shadows stretched out from the fronts of the buildings along the street. The men and ladies of the night would be awake and stretching. Chad glanced at the brass clock and, feeling a little guilty about it, went to rouse Starr for his night shift.

Before he left the office, Chad took a rifle from the rack. He had the feeling that he'd be better off carrying one from now on. Walking to the stable, his eyes studying the streets, he claimed his buckskin horse and swung into the saddle.

'They ever pay you for these horses?' Chad asked the stableman.

'Yes, sir, Marshal. Mr Walker took care of that.'

'Walker? He seems to have a pretty good grip on the town's purse strings, doesn't he?'

The man shrugged his scrawny shoulders. It made no difference to him, obviously, so long as he was paid.

Chad kneed the horse and made his way toward the pueblo, taking a slightly different route from the one he had ridden the night before. He wouldn't care to get ambushed again. After putting his horse away he washed off at the pump, then went in. He could smell something cooking; somehow he had not been hungry all day, now he was.

There was a place set for him at the kitchen table. It seemed he would be eating alone. The aunts, he knew, ate by themselves. Candida was nowhere to be seen. Her absence took some of the flavor out of the meal for him, but he enjoyed two chicken *tamales, frijoles* and Spanish rice. Finished, he thanked the aunts and walked into the main room, still hoping to come across Candida. At length he opened the front door and stepped out onto the porch, hoping he was not offering some lurking sniper a silhouette to aim at. Staying alive in Los Palmas was becoming more chancy with each passing day.

What would tomorrow and the day after bring, once word got around what he was up to? He thought again of Candida's advice to just ride away from the town. He thought again of Candida. The girl must have been closed away in her room. Chad decided that the best thing he could do was to turn in early, as he had the night before. Still he stood at the open window of his room, staring out at the purple dusk for a long while before, almost angrily, he shucked his boots and climbed into bed.

Morning found him awake in the gray of pre-dawn once more. Well-fed, well-rested, there was nevertheless an uneasiness in him. He dressed, buckled on his Colt revolver and slipped out of the house again, starting for the canyon. The goat kept in the back yard did not feel as feisty this morning, it seemed, for it stayed well away from Chad, munching on tufts of brown grass.

The goat had nothing to concern him, though it should have. Chad knew that *chivo* – goat meat – was considered the tastiest for *tacos, enchiladas,* almost anything the aunts wished to use it for, after it had been roasted in a covered pit. The goat munched on, unaware of its future fate. Chad's stride, on the other hand, was heavy. It almost felt as if he were climbing the steps to a scaffold he had constructed for himself.

Making his way down into the canyon he again went beneath the cottonwood trees, their tips now shining silver in the light of the rising new sun. After four practice draws, Chad focused his attention on the white rock on the bluff that he had been using as a target. His draw felt much smoother this morning, and as he emptied to pistol white dust sprayed into the air.

'I think you got him twice,' Candida said from behind him. She crept forward from the shade of the trees as Chad reloaded.

'Who?' Chad muttered. How did she manage to sneak up on him like that?

'Glen Walker, of course,' Candida said lightly, striking the same pose as she had a day earlier, one foot raised behind her, against the trunk of the tree.

'I'm not doing this because I mean to kill Glen Walker,' Chad said with annoyance.

'I already told you, you will have to. But you still need more practice.'

Then she turned and walked away lightly, leaving Chad grinding his teeth as he watched her easy stride and sway.

*

It took a good half-minute of rapping on the door before Ben Cody swung it in. He wore a white apron again. There was the pleasant smell of cornbread baking inside the house. Cody admitted that was what it was.

'I thought I'd give it a try. A man can only eat so many eggs before he tires of them. Follow me into the kitchen – coffee's boiling.'

Seated at the kitchen table, Chad watched as Cody opened the oven door and used a pair of towels to remove the tin tray from it. The cornbread was steaming, and Chad couldn't deny that it smelled appetizing. He told Cody as much.

'Well, when my wife used to make it, it seemed to rise more. I'm still learning.' As he was talking, he used a knife the size of a trowel to slather butter on the cornbread. 'I'm going to have buttermilk with mine,' Cody said. 'Want some?'

'No, thanks. Coffee is fine for me.'

Cut into generous squares the hot cornbread was placed on a platter and served. Chad let it cool for a minute and then dived in. It was good, very good and he took three squares, following it with Cody's coffee. Cody himself didn't look as if he were going to quit until the entire stack of cornbread was gone. Chad let the former marshal finish what he wanted before opening the conversation.

'I've come over here because I need to know a few things, Cody. First off, are there any honest men on the town council?'

'Reg Hicks is a good man. He didn't go along with the vote on the new tax. He's a lawyer, but still a decent enough sort.'

'I'll talk to him,' Chad said. Cody's eyes narrowed. He wiped at his mouth with a napkin.

'You're up to something,' Cody said.

'I think I will be, but I'll need some help.' Chad took another sip of his coffee. 'Tell me, Cody, how did Glen Walker ever gain so much power in Las Palmas?'

'Well,' Cody leaned back in his chair, hands on his expansive belly, 'most of the town council members have their own businesses, regular jobs to attend to. Someone – probably Glen Walker himself – proposed that they hire a town manager to handle the day-to-day affairs of the town, leaving them free to go about their own business. That's where Glen Walker's authority comes from. I guess over time they just sort of forgot about being councilmen altogether and let Walker pretty much manage the town's affairs the way he wanted to.'

'I see,' Chad said, although he didn't, really. Those men had been elected to do a job, but they seemed to just be a rubber stamp for the policies of the mayor and Glen Walker.

'Sometimes people just want an elected position

for the prestige they think it gives them; they don't really care about the job itself,' Cody said with the voice of experience.

'What about Mayor Swanson? Certainly he was aware of Walker's maneuvering?'

'I'm sorry to say the man is greedy and lazy, but he gives good campaign speeches and has a nice smile.'

'And Judge Lambert?'

'Well, he was appointed by the county circuit court. He generally does what he thinks will appease everyone else. Also,' Cody said with a wink, 'he's Swanson's brother-in-law.'

Chad rose and walked to the kitchen window. The goat, untethered, still wandered the yard. 'You said the outlying ranchers won't stand for the new tax.'

'I don't think so,' Cody said with a heavy shake of his head, 'and the only way to collect from them would be to take a small army onto their ranges. Some of those ranchers have twenty, thirty hands working for them.'

'What was Glen Walker planning to do about them?' Chad asked, turning back toward Cody.

'Probably nothing right away, although he does have his own band of paid men: Skinny Jim Foote, Lloyd Pearson, Randall Hart . . . a few others. As long as he could collect the taxes in Las Palmas he'd let the ranchers slide, for a year or so, maybe. But at some point Judge Lambert could probably find a way to throw a lien on the ranches and even seize them – if they could.'

'That would be some commotion.'

'That doesn't even begin to cover it, Dempster. It would be an out and out bloody range war.'

'Who's the biggest rancher around?'

'Art Spykes of Wagonwheel Ranch.'

'Do you get along with him?' Chad asked.

'We've never had any problems between us, outside of a few times his men came into town intent on getting as drunk as possible and I had to lock some of them up. Why?'

'I was hoping I could persuade you to talk to him and let him know what's brewing, if he doesn't already know.'

Cody stretched his arms over his head and answered, 'I suppose it's not a bad day for a buggy ride. I haven't been moving around much these last few days. But tell me, Dempster, what good would it do to talk to Spykes?'

'Maybe none. I just think the ranchers ought to know that they may have to fight for their land. I want them to know that the law is on their side.'

'But the law isn't, Dempster,' Cody said with a frown. 'You may be on their side, but that little piece of paper that's been attached to the town ordinances carries a lot more weight than one man with a badge.'

'I know that, that's what makes this whole situation so tricky. But I've made up my mind; I'm siding with the people and not the town hall. What can they do? Fire me?'

Cody was still frowning deeply. 'Glen Walker wouldn't be willing to let it go at that, Dempster. He is going to take it very personally if you even look like you're standing in the way of his plans.'

'I'll keep practicing,' Chad said. The comment made no sense to Cody, but the former marshal let it slide. He rose heavily to his feet.

'Well, I suppose I'd better wash up and get my buggy ready. It's going to be a hot day, and Wagonwheel is quite a way to drive in the sun. What are you planning to do, Dempster?' he asked as he again walked Chad to the front door.

'First of all, I mean to look up this Reg Hicks and ask just how many of the town council members actually approved the new tax law. You say he's a lawyer: he might have some idea of how it can be legally stopped before Las Palmas is running with blood.'

'You're planning to start a war,' Cody said once they reached the front porch.

'No, sir, not at all. I'm just trying to figure out a way to survive one.'

NINE

The low sun had risen enough to glint brilliantly through the creekside trees. Chad Dempster had much on his mind as he started back toward Las Palmas. Had he suddenly gone mad? To even think of trying to stop Glen Walker seemed insane. Yet he felt an obligation to this town and its citizens, most of whom he had never even met. People had the right to feel that the law was working for them and not against them.

Right now he was still the law.

He dipped down into a sandy crossing that forded the narrow stream. The water flowed prettily in the morning light. Silver-bright and sparkling.

The gunman opened up on him as he reached midstream. The buckskin reared up, then settled again as a pair of bullets whistled past. Chad heeled the horse for the far bank, which was dotted with willows along the sandy beach. He swung down before the buckskin had quit running and, rifle in hand, dove for the ground beneath the willow brush as another bullet sheared twigs around him in its passing.

It was silent then. Chad lay still against the sand of the river beach. A few slender shadows from the sun behind the willows lightly stained the earth. He saw no one moving. He could hear only the buckskin horse, apparently calmed, munching on tender willow shoots.

He did not dare move. His attacker had apparently lost sight of him and he didn't care to give the sniper a clue as to where he lay. His only movement had been to prop himself up on his elbows to give himself a prone firing position. But there was no target. The sun rose higher, a slight, warm breeze wove its way through the silver-green foliage of the willows. Still he waited. Sweat trickled into his eyes.

Whoever had shot at him had not risked this much to simply ride away now. He was waiting for Chad to move, to try to recover his horse. Another half an hour passed as the sun grew hotter. Chad began to believe that he was wrong, that the sniper had pulled out. But he had heard no horse moving away from the creek bottom, and horses are not very good at tiptoeing.

He saw a shadow moving beyond the screen of willows. Just for a second or two. It seemed to be creeping toward him. A man in a crouch, coming his way. Chad's mouth was dry; his body was bathed in sweat. Minutes passed without anything happening. Had he been mistaken about the ghostly shadow? He blinked the perspiration from his eyes. The buckskin shuffled its feet and Chad glanced that way. His horse had its ears pricked; it was looking in the direction in which Chad had seen movement. He steadied himself behind the sights of his Winchester.

There was a sudden burst of fire from the willows. Sand kicked up around Chad as three shots were fired in his direction. Chad fired at the muzzle blast he had seen, levering four bullets from his own rifle through the barrel. He saw the mysterious shadow rear up, wave its arms and fall back, its rifle falling free. Chad waited long minutes, not wanting to rise if the man still lived.

He did not. After what seemed an hour but was probably only a few minutes, Chad rose slowly and made his way through the heavy brush to the spot where the sniper lay dead. He had never seen Lloyd Pearson before, so he could give no name to the dark-faced man who lay there, mouth gaping, eyes open to the sunlight that filtered through the surrounding trees. It made no difference. He knew where the sniper had gotten his orders, and Chad felt a cool shiver pass through his bones.

How many other men whom he had never even seen were out there, waiting to kill him?

Domino Jones smiled sourly as the tall man approached him at the bar in FitzRoy's where he was just finishing his third whiskey. He watched Glen Walker in the mirror behind the distorting ranks of liquor bottles.

'What the hell do you want?' he growled at Walker.

'Take it easy, Domino. I've never done anything to you, and I might be in a position to do you a large favor.' Walker signaled to the bartender for a drink, and leaned up on the bar, his elbows planted on the scarred dark wood.

Domino Jones did not hate Glen Walker so much as darkly envy him. Walker had himself a classy little woman. He was always barbered, always wearing fine clothes like the ivory-colored suit he had on now. He had always had his way in Las Palmas. Domino Jones was just a street thug in a ratty red flannel shirt and greasy blue jeans. Right now he still wore his right arm in a sling. To top that there was still some talk of trying him for the attempted murder of Tanglefoot.

'It's time for us to clear up some matters,' Glen Walker said, drinking his whiskey. He looked around to make sure there was no one in earshot. At this time of the morning they pretty much had the place to themselves.

119

'What are you talking about?' Domino asked, baffled.

'I made a mistake,' Walker said, turning to lean his back against the bar. He smiled that ingratiating smile of his. He lowered his voice, 'The marshal has to go.'

'Tanglefoot!' Domino Jones said in disbelief. 'You practically nursed and burped him.'

'I told you – I made a mistake. Can you handle it?'

Domino's eyes glittered with dark suspicion. 'Why me?'

'Because I'm asking you to. I can't be involved. Besides, there may be something in it for you – a lot of something.'

'Like what?' Jones growled, finishing his own drink.

'Like getting that attempted murder count against you dropped.'

'By actually killing him?'

'That's right. Handle it with no witnesses around; get yourself an alibi set up. I'll have the original charge taken care of.'

'Judge Lambert don't seem to want to let that go.' Domino wagged his head.

'Domino,' Glen Walker said with a smile as he placed his hand on the big man's shoulder, 'don't give it a thought. Whose pocket do you think the judge is in?'

Byron Starr didn't stagger into the marshal's office until 9.30 that morning. Chad supposed his deputy had been involved in a long conversation with Peggy Kimball. Starr didn't look particularly unhappy, just weary.

'Sorry, boss,' Starr said, forcing a smile.

'For what? I don't care what time you get off so long as you're here when you're supposed to take over for me.' Chad stood near his desk, trying to get some of the dust off his clothes with a whisk broom. Starr frowned.

'Did you have a bad morning already?'

'I've had better.' Chad decided not to tell Starr about the sniper just then. That was over with, and Starr already knew they had enemies in town. Just not how many.

'Did you see Jones or Deacon Forge around?' Chad asked as Starr slipped out of his jacket with a yawn.

'Not Forge, but Domino was in the FitzRoy when I left. We ignored each other.'

'Let's hope he continues to act that way,' Chad said.

'Why wouldn't he? What's he going to profit by continuing matters?'

Chad shrugged. He couldn't think of a thing, but you never knew what was going on in a man's mind.

He told Byron Starr: 'Grab yourself some sleep. You might want to drop the bar across the door – I'm going to be going out for a while.'

'Important business?'

'I hope so,' Chad answered.

It wasn't hard to find Reg Hicks's office. Half a block along the plankwalk beyond the court-house stood a narrow yellow clapboard building with a sign hanging from the awning. 'Reginald Hicks, Attorney at Law. Thomas Raymond, Notary Public.' Chad entered the small office and walked across the floor to one of the open doors within. A thin blond man with a pen in his hand glanced up, his blue eyes appearing large through the lenses of the round gold-rimmed spectacles he wore.

'Mr Hicks?' Chad asked. Hicks's sharp eyes had already caught the gleam of the badge on Chad's shirt front.

'Yes. Come in, Marshal, and tell me what I can do for you.'

'I'm not sure that I know what you can do for me,' Chad said, seating himself at Hicks's gesture. He leaned forward, holding his hat in his hands. 'I was just hoping that there's something.' He was silent a second, taking a deep breath as he studied the pale-haired man. 'Ben Cody says that you're an honest man,' he blurted out.

Hicks removed his spectacles, polished them on a soft square of rag he kept in his desk for that purpose, replaced them and asked in a low voice, 'Is this about the new tax?'

'Yes, sir.'

Hicks drummed his fingertips on his desktop. 'I was hoping you might come by about that. Rather, I was hoping you would. I have no knowledge of who you are, know nothing about you or your ambitions.'

'Ambitions?' Chad repeated slowly. 'I don't suppose I have any except to protect this town, which is what I was hired to do.' Hicks studied Chad for a long minute while Chad was thinking about what he should say next.

'All right, here it is,' Chad said, leaning still further forward. 'This new tax is going to make a lot of people in town mad. I need to know this: is it legal?'

'Legal, yes. Moral, ethical, no.'

'You were there when the vote was taken by the council, I understand,' Chad said. 'You voted against it, didn't you?'

Hicks nodded. 'I did, and so did Kennedy and Walsh.'

'But then . . . how many members does the council have?'

'Five.'

'Then you had the majority, so how. . . ?'

'Mayor Swanson stepped in. I won't say he was angry, but he was upset. He said that according to the town charter, he was allowed to vote. He voted for enactment.'

'That still left you with a tie vote.'

'Yes,' Hicks said, 'and the matter was sent up to Judge Lambert for a final decision.'

'Swanson's brother-in-law.'

'That's right,' Hicks said. Then he shrugged slightly. 'Stinks, doesn't it?'

Chad shook his head in wonder. 'You people have a strange way of doing business.'

A little defensively, Hicks replied. 'We didn't have the time – the days, weeks to invest in debating the law. Kennedy owns the lumberyard, Walsh the hardware store. They couldn't close down for weeks while this dragged on. None of us thought the law could be enforced anyway. Ben Cody? He was so close to retirement that he wouldn't walk across the street to try do so.

'I suppose,' Hicks went on in a more thoughtful tone, 'that we should have known that Glen Walker would be on the lookout for someone to replace Cody.'

'Me,' Chad was forced to admit. 'Just a fool who'd do what he was told.'

'But you're refusing to do it?'

'Walk into the Clipper or FitzRoy and tell them they have to pay five per cent of their take to us for law enforcement from now on? No. I'd be more of threat to them than anyone I was supposed to be protecting them against. Except that I'd be robbing them legally. Who will they blame? Not the mayor, the judge, not Glen Walker, but the man who comes in and demands money from them. I'd have a target on my back in this town.'

'I suppose,' Hicks said. He was lost in his own thoughts. He removed his spectacles again and rubbed his eyes. 'So you intend to try to stand up against Walker and his crew?'

'I'd be a renegade lawman they'd feel justified in getting rid of, wouldn't I? Tell me, Hicks, how many men does Walker have working for him? Thugs, I mean.'

'I couldn't say exactly. There's Skinny Jim Foote, his chief gunman. Randall Hart and Lloyd Pearson that I know of. There could be a dozen I don't know about.'

'I'll be a marked man,' Chad said. He probably already was. He had been shot at twice from ambush and he knew that Walker had already approached Starr about taking his job.

Listen to Candida – ride out of town, and now! You can't win this fight, he told himself, and it's not really even your fight.

A stray beam of morning sunlight glinted off his badge and reflected off Hicks's spectacles.

'Can you help me out, Hicks? Are you willing to?'

'How? What can I do?' Hicks spread his hands.

'That's what I'm here to ask you. You're the one with the law degree. Can't we get that law off the books before the trouble really begins? Can't you think of a way to get rid of the mayor and Judge Lambert?'

'And of course, Glen Walker?'

'Leave Glen Walker to me,' Chad said, for again Candida had been right, clever woman that she was. *You will have to kill Glen Walker.*

'Have you any ideas?' Chad asked, pursuing the thought. 'Because if something isn't done about this law, the streets will be running with blood. You, me, everyone else who's threatened might just as well leave town now, tails between our legs, because when it's time to enforce the new taxes, people will start shooting. I don't think that's the kind of town you want to live in.'

'We could force a referendum on the ordinance,' Hicks said. 'We could also seek a recall vote on Mayor Swanson. As for the judge – he's an appointee of the circuit court. We could petition for his impeachment on the grounds of malfeasance.'

'You could do all that?'

'Yes, or I could just thrust my head into a thresh-ing machine,' Hicks said, obviously upset now. 'How long do you think they'd let me live if they found out I was carrying on such legal maneuver-ing?'

'I don't know.' Chad rose from his chair and planted his hat on his head. 'All right, then. It's all up to you then, Mr Hicks. It's your town, not mine. If you don't care enough to take the risks needed to keep it clean, I can't make you.'

With that Chad started toward the door, feeling neither defeated nor victorious. He had made a try. That was all he could do.

As he reached the front door he heard Hicks call to him weakly.

'Listen, Marshal. . . .'

But Chad thought he had done all the listening that he was capable of. Either Hicks's conscience would prod him to do the right thing, or he would simply take the easy route, satisfying himself that there was really nothing he could accomplish anyway.

And what was there that Chad could really accomplish against this stacked deal? The air outside was stagnant and dry. It had the stink of corruption about it. The streets were nearly empty as the temperature continued to climb across the desert community. His buckskin horse was still hitched in front of the marshal's office, its head hanging, miserable under the weight of the high sun. Chad decided to stable the animal, where it would at least have shade and water. The horse was right:

It was not the sort of day to strike out across the

long desert. It was only the concept and not the reality that seemed alluring.

TEN

The front door to the jailhouse was unbarred when Chad returned from stabling his horse. Apparently Starr had not felt concerned about his own safety. Or maybe he had just staggered off to bed without remembering to do it. Chad smiled faintly. These nightly conversations Starr was having with Peggy Kimball seemed to be wearing his deputy down.

Chad entered the office, leaving the door open behind him. There was the slightest of breezes rising and he thought it might cool things off a bit. No sooner had he stepped inside than Starr appeared from the back room, where he had his cot.

'I am going to find a way to get me a place to live somewhere no matter what it takes,' Starr said in a sleep-mutter. 'Is there any water in that barrel?'

He walked to the small oaken barrel that they used chiefly to store water to boil for coffee. He used the dipper to take a drink. The remainder of the water in the dipper he splashed over his head. He turned toward Chad. 'You've been gone a while, Marshal. What've you been doing.'

'Getting us in more trouble, I suppose,' Chad answered.

'Oh? Why don't you just give it up, Chad? You're not cut out for this, and you know it.'

'You want my job?' Chad asked.

'Maybe I do,' Starr answered. He leaned back against the counter. 'I mean, maybe I *should* want it. Peggy was asking me when I thought we could move in together, when I could get her out of the saloon business. I think she has been talking to Glen Walker again about what an opportunity I had.'

'There's only one person with an opportunity in Las Palmas – and that's Glen Walker,' Chad answered.

'Well, by God!' Starr snarled. His eyes went narrow and he drew and fired his Colt before Chad could have touched his own pistol. From behind him Chad heard a moan, the whimper of a crippled animal, and he spun around in confusion, seeing Domino Jones – dead – against the office floor, a gun trickling free of his grip.

'Starr!' Chad said, still trying to catch his breath.

For a moment there, he thought his frustrated deputy had turned on him, turned violently. He turned to find Starr holstering his pistol, his head still damp, his eyes still bleary.

'That's one less of them,' Starr muttered, then he started back toward his cot in the storeroom.

Chad stood over the body of Domino Jones. A few passers-by had stopped to peer into the office, summoned by the sound of gunfire. How many times did that make it that Starr had saved his life? He remembered Starr's words: *You're not really cut out for this, and you know it.*

'I'll keep practicing,' he said to no one. Then to the group of men standing in the doorway, 'I want you to get this man out of here. The town will pay you two dollars each for the job.'

Would they? Who knew? And Chad did not care; he just wanted the late, abominable Domino Jones taken out of his sight.

But the man remained in his memory as he seated himself at his desk again.

Glen Walker was muttering to himself as he walked back to his hotel and entered the room. Carmalita was there on the bed – where else would she be? He took off his coat and flung it aside. Then he walked to the window and stared out at the sun-beaten town of Las Palmas.

That stupid Domino Jones had gotten drunk and

had chosen to just walk right into the marshal's office and brace him there. And gotten himself gunned down. The idiot! Chad Dempster must be better with a gun than Walker had given him credit for. He had gotten Charlie Burnett the day he had also winged Domino in the alley. Randall Hart had missed him when he was sent to eliminate Dempster on his way home. Lloyd Pearson had not returned from the job he had been given.

Now Domino Jones. Maybe Skinny Jim could take him: he was quick on the draw, but Walker had started to think he would have to get rid of the man himself.

With that thought in his mind he retrieved his rolled-up gunbelt and Colt revolver from the top shelf of the closet and sat down at the table to clean and oil the pistol while Carmalita, sitting up against the pillows, watched him with wide, dark eyes.

'I thought you didn't do that no more,' she said uneasily. 'You said no more shooting, that there were easier ways for us to make money.'

'Good help is hard to come by,' Walker growled.

'Send out the Skinny Jimmy,' Carmalita said, swinging her legs to the side of the bed, watching him with concern.

'I probably will let him take a try,' Walker answered, cleaning the muzzle of the pistol with a small brass brush. 'But I have a feeling that this is going to come down to him and me eventually.'

'Who is *him*?' she asked although she thought she already knew the answer. She crossed the room to sit down facing Glen Walker as he checked the action on the pistol, then slowly began loading six brass cartridges into the chambers. 'You are talking about Tangletoes, aren't you?'

'Marshal Charles Proctor Dempster,' Glen Walker said glumly, slapping the loading gate of the revolver shut and holstering it. 'He's just gotten to be too much to handle. He's been seen out at Ben Cody's place, and visiting Reg Hicks.'

'Who?'

'The lawyer who sits on the town council. I don't know what those two are cooking up, but Charles Dempster has gotten out of hand. I regret the day I ever hatched the plan involving him – don't say anything, Carmalita!'

'I wasn't – not about that.' She leaned across the table and took his hand. 'But do you have to kill him? My cousin, Candida, she had grown very fond of this man.'

'That's no reason not to take care of business,' Walker snapped, rising to place his gun away for the time being. With his back to Carmalita, he said, 'Or have you forgotten all the plans we have made – a grand house with servants, a surrey and a matched set of bay horses, furs and silks and satins to wrap yourself in?'

'I have forgotten none of it,' Carmalita said. 'And

133

I will always appreciate it. But, Glen, sometimes plans go wrong.'

'Not this one,' Glen Walker said in what was nearly a snarl. 'I won't let this one go wrong, and as for Candida, well, it's just too bad for her. I'll be back after lunch. I need to talk to the mayor and Judge Lambert and let them know that Hicks might be trying to stick his nose into our business as well.'

He went out and closed the door firmly. Carmalita sat on her bed in her night clothes, staring after him.

'Poor Candida,' she said aloud. 'Poor Candida.'

Jim Foote sat gloomily at a round table in the corner of the Clipper saloon. It had been a long time since he was thin, but the name 'Skinny Jim' had stuck to him, and they would probably still call him that if he gained so much weight that he resembled Ben Cody. The saloon was crowded, as it always was when the desert sun drifted high.

Foote was in the dumps because he had just gotten word that his closest friend and long-time saddle partner, Lloyd Pearson, had been found shot dead up along Lindo Creek. Rumor had it that the marshal, Dempster, must have done it. Skinny Jim didn't see how it could have happened that way. Lloyd was a very careful man.

Jim sipped at his beer, not really tasting it.

Around him was the noisy, constant turmoil of the Clipper saloon crowd. It was irritating to a man in his mood. One voice in particular offended him.

'It's only twenty bucks, Biggs,' Deacon Forge was whining. 'You know I'm good for twenty.'

Foote glanced that way. Deacon Forge sat at a four-man poker game, his cards folded together in front of his chin.

'Hell, you don't even have a job any more,' Aaron Biggs, a big, red-faced man replied. 'I wouldn't take your marker for a dime.'

'Just take my IOU,' Forge was pleading. He might have thought he had a good hand, but he seemed to have forgotten that you have to pay to play. His voice was irritating Skinny Jim. When Forge thought he was riding high he had come in here every night to gamble. Twice, while he was still deputy marshal, Deacon Forge had arrested Skinny Jim, both times ruining a night Jim had planned. Skinny Jim couldn't stand the man, especially not today.

'I'll put my horse up,' Forge was saying.

'I've got a horse,' Aaron Biggs said. 'I come in here to play for cash – which I am a little short on.'

'You've got to listen to me!' Deacon Forge said, getting to his feet.

'Everyone's getting damned tired of listening to you,' Skinny Jim said, rising as well. 'You're a lousy gambler, you were a rotten deputy, and you're not much of a man. I don't know why they even tolerate you in here.'

'Shut up, Foote!' Deacon Forge said.

'Did you actually say that to me?' Skinny Jim said, walking nearer to the card table as other men backed away.

'You heard me.'

'I heard you, but I didn't like it. Back away from that table, Deke. I'd hate to accidentally hit one of the boys.'

'You've got to be kidding,' Deacon Forge said, placing his cards down on the table. Forge was good with a gun, but the alcohol he had consumed gave him an inflated idea of how good. Everyone knew that Skinny Jim was the fastest gun in Las Palmas.

'I'll tell you when it's a joke,' Skinny Jim Foote said coldly. 'Draw or run!'

'By God, then! You asked for it.' Deacon Forge went for his Colt. He drew first, but Skinny Jim lived up to his reputation. His pistol banged off a shot just as Forge pulled the trigger on his own gun. Smoke curled up toward the ceiling of the Clipper as men dove for cover, the sound of the sudden shots still echoing in their ears. . . .

Chad Dempster happened to be passing by the Clipper at that very moment. The gunfire sent him racing through the door. He could not tell what was going on. Men milled around, looked up from under overturned tables or hid behind the bar. He fired his own revolver into the ceiling to try to calm things down.

Somehow it worked. Men sat on the floor or pressed their backs against the walls, staring at the man with the badge. Chad crossed the room slowly. He looked down at the still forms of Skinny Jim and Deacon Forge.

'Someone get them out of here,' he said. 'The town will pay you two dollars apiece for helping.' Then, gun smoke burning his nostrils, Chad walked through the swinging doors and out onto the porch, breathing in fresh air. He leaned against the outside wall and ejected the spent cartridge from his Colt, replacing it with a shell from his gunbelt loops. A scrawny man in a badly frayed twill jacket had emerged from the saloon. His eyes were bleary, his legs unsteady beneath him.

'They were both troublemakers,' the man said, his eyes bright with liquor. 'You done this town a favor. That was good shooting in there.'

There was a surge of men rushing toward the Clipper, drawn by the shots. Chad saw the little drunk walk toward the excited newcomers and point back at him. He was waving his arms and talking up a storm and the men who had not been there seemed to be soaking it up. A rumor had been born and before nightfall even those who had actually witnessed what had happened were challenged in their memories. The rumor became fact before the sun had gone down.

'All right,' Glen Walker said as he strapped on his sidearm. 'Enough is enough.'

Carmalita, who had actually found the energy to stir from the bed and put on her dark-blue dress in hopes of being invited out to dinner, stared at Glen as he buckled the gun on. 'What do you mean?' she asked, her voice a little tremulous.

'I was just telling you. Don't you ever listen? Charles Dempster shot both Deacon Forge and Skinny Jim dead over at the Clipper.'

'The tangled-legs man killed Skinny Jimmy?' an astonished Carmalita asked. 'You always tell me Skinny Jimmy is the best of your men.'

'He was,' Walker said without expression. 'I don't know how it happened, but everyone in town is talking about it. He got both of them!'

'So now it is up to you,' Carmalita said.

'It looks like it,' Glen Walker answered. 'I don't know what road the man is following, but I know where it's going to end.'

'Are we going out to dinner?' Carmalita asked, stepping near to Glen Walker, plucking at his coat sleeves. He grinned down at the simple woman.

'Sure,' he said. 'Why not?'

'They're calling you a real town-tamer,' Byron Starr said in the jailhouse office. He was smiling, but

Chad Dempster wore a heavy frown.

'I told you what happened, Starr. I don't know how the story got so twisted.'

'Don't complain about it,' Starr advised him. 'It could work to your advantage. Men will think twice about pulling a gun on you.'

'I don't think anyone in this town thinks at all,' Chad said, tilting back in his chair, hands clasped behind his head. He glanced at the wall clock. A quarter to eight. Nearly time for Starr to begin his rounds.

'You may be right, but look at it this way, Chad: we've got two more of the enemy out of the way.'

'Three if you count Domino Jones,' Chad said, mulling that. 'But how many are left out there? I've heard that Glen Walker can easily raise a dozen men.'

'Well, we'll just have to take care of business as it comes up. No sense worrying ourselves sick about every possibility.'

'No, I suppose you're right.' Chad sighed and leaned forward, placing his hands on his desk.

'Do you think this Reg Hicks is going to help us out any?' Starr asked. 'Sooner or later we're going to have to start collecting taxes or get thrown out on our ears.'

'I don't know what he's going to do. He may not be inclined to try, or he just might not be able to do anything.'

'I hope he can get something done,' Starr said, reaching for his hat. 'This town would settle down and be a fair place to live if the tax code went back to the way it used to be.'

'You sound like you're thinking of staying here,' Chad said as he watched Starr adjust his gunbelt.

'Maybe I am. I could find myself in worse situations.'

'And you could still find the county sheriff on your doorstep.'

Starr froze his movements. His eyes went hard. 'Don't think I'm not aware of that, Chad. Some sins ride with a man his whole life, don't they?'

Without waiting for an answer, Starr turned, walked through the door and out onto the sundown streets of Las Palmas.

Chad was not far behind him. He was tired and hungry. Candida would be there at the end of his ride home. Or would she? The bright-eyed little woman had not been there to join him at the dinner table the night before. Was she cooling off toward him?

Perhaps she had never held any feelings at all for Chad. Maybe it was all in his imagination. He hadn't known many women and it was difficult for him to judge. She might have just been being friendly because they shared a house. He might have unknowingly given her some hint of how he felt about her, a hint that had caused her to back away from him.

Stepping into the buckskin's saddle he forced thoughts of Candida away and returned his thinking to the problems of the town.

He got no further thinking about that than he had with his thoughts of Candida. No matter how he was trying, he still did not know enough about the politics and connections of the men in Las Palmas even to know who was who. Who among them were Walker men? Anyone could walk up to him on the street to shake his hand, then pull out a pistol while he was smiling at him. He supposed that Ben Cody would know their faces and the affiliations of almost any man in town, but Ben Cody's time had come and gone, primarily because of his knowledge of the way the town worked.

Chad shook his head and shifted his thoughts again. The sky had changed. On his ride home there was a sheer purple veil of cloud overhead, pierced by pinpoints of silver stars. It would be a pleasant evening, in other times, in which to sit on the front porch until night settled and the air cooled. If a man had someone to sit there with.

Gloomily he rode on, approaching the adobe house. He had not really accomplished anything on this day. He somehow doubted that Candida would be there to welcome him. And he knew with certainty that Byron Starr had been correct.

If they did not soon start collecting the new taxes, they would be out on their ears and a new batch of men, willing to work only for the money, would be brought in to take their places. Then the war for Las Palmas would begin in earnest.

ELEVEN

The new sun was angled so low that its beams only struck the ceiling and the roof beams in Chad's bedroom the next morning. It was very early, but he had accustomed himself to rising early by now. He yawned, glanced at his open window and smiled. A bold mockingbird had perched on the ledge and was now hopping back and forth as if trying to decide whether or not to enter the room.

'You wouldn't like it here,' Chad growled as he rose, and the bird gave a single squawk before flying away on white-banded wings.

He dressed morosely. He had again not seen Candida the evening before, although he had heard her talking somewhere in the house. Pulling on his shirt, Chad wondered once more what he might have done to drive her away.

There was something simmering in a huge black kettle in the kitchen, but neither of the aunts was around. Unhappily, Chad crossed the yard and headed toward the canyon. The goat, now tethered, watched his progress. Slipping down the bank of the canyon wall, he again went to his practice range. His improvement had been steady but slow, and Chad figured he could still use all the practice he could get.

He drew and fired at the white rock. Drew and fired twice. Drew again and fired. He watched with satisfaction as the white dust from the rock drifted away in the wind. He turned toward where Candida had been standing the past two mornings, wanting to ask for her approval. But she was not there. It was as if she had vanished from his life.

Chad could smell coffee boiling even before he swung down from the buckskin in front of Ben Cody's neat little white house. As he approached the door he caught the scent of pork sausage frying. Ben Cody, in his apron, answered the door before Chad had knocked. He carried a huge yellow mixing bowl and a wooden spoon.

'I heard your horse,' Cody told him. 'Besides, I'm getting used to you coming by at breakfast time. I thought I'd try my hand at sausage and hotcakes this morning.' He stirred the batter in the yellow bowl. 'Want to give it a try?'

'No, thanks, Cody. Just coffee if you don't mind. I came by to see what you've found out.'

In the kitchen, Cody poured Chad a steaming cup of coffee and returned to his batter mixing. 'Well, this is the way it's going to go, Marshal,' Cody said, dribbling the batter onto a hot steel sheet where it formed six small hotcakes, 'I talked to Art Spykes over at the Wagonwheel yesterday, and he's more than a little peeved about the new tax law. He's willing to back you up if you're willing to take on Glen Walker, Mayor Swanson and Judge Lambert.'

'I'm going to give it a try. A lot depends on Reg Hicks.'

'He'll go along with you,' Cody said, flipping the griddle cakes over. 'Hicks is not a brave man, but he's a decent one. I'm sure he must have been a little reluctant. But it was a lot to dump in his lap at once.'

'I can see that,' Chad said, sipping at his coffee. 'What help does Art Spykes think he can be?'

'I'm supposed to tell you that,' Cody said, looking at the underside of the hotcakes. Assured that they were cooked well enough, he took his spatula and shoveled them onto a large platter before arranging six more dollops of batter to form replacements for them. Chad waited patiently.

'Art's sending ten or twelve of his men into Las Palmas, to watch things until this is over one way or the other. If Reg Hicks can organize a recall election, everything might just work out. But if Glen

Walker takes to the streets with all of his men, no one is going to come out to vote.'

'I guess not,' Chad acknowledged. He hadn't really thought of that. 'Look, Cody, I don't know any of the Wagonwheel riders either. How will I recognize them, and what will they be doing?'

'Spykes thought of that. He's going to have all of his men wearing identical red bandannas. They'll spread themselves out along the main street, at every corner, just keeping their eyes open.' Cody smiled and flipped the new batch of hotcakes. 'We wouldn't want anybody gunning down our new marshal on the eve of the election.'

'No,' Chad answered numbly. 'We wouldn't want that.'

'So get along now, Dempster, if you don't want to eat. You've got a town to nursemaid and a dozen volunteer deputies to help you keep it safe until the new elections.'

'If this all works out. . . .' Chad said rising from his chair.

'Even if it doesn't, no one can say you didn't give it your best shot, *Marshal.*'

Back at the office Starr was still awake and alert. Chad told him what was happening.

'I was wondering,' Byron Starr said. 'Just as I reached the office I saw a group of cowhands drifting into town in twos and threes. It seemed sort of strange to me, so I watched them for a while, wondering if they were some wild bunch with an idea of trying to tree this town, but they just sort of fanned out. Later I saw them standing on the corners up and down the street. I'd never seen anything like that and I almost asked them who the hell they were, but I thought I'd better let you handle it.

'And now that you mention it, that is what caught my eye – every single one was wearing a red kerchief around his neck.'

'You'd better get some sleep,' Chad suggested.

'Not today,' Starr objected. 'It seems there's going to be a lot happening.'

They heard a tentative knock on the doorframe and turned to find Reg Hicks standing there, his face flushed. The blue eyes behind his spectacles looked excited and fearful at once. 'Well, here you are,' the lawyer said and handed Chad a bulletin with the bold heading:

SPECIAL ELECTION

Chad sat down at his desk and scanned the bulletin. Ballots could be obtained at the courthouse that morning for a key vote on an initiative to reject the new business tax, as well as whether or not the people wished to retain Mayor Swanson or recall him.

'It didn't take you long to get moving on this

after you made up your mind,' Chad said, handing the bulletin to Starr to read.

'Not once I got hold of Kennedy and Walsh, the other councilmen who voted against the ordinance in the first place. They've both been feeling miserable about the way the law was passed, how it looked for them.

'Can the mayor pull the same trick as he did last time?'

'Not while he's under the shadow of a recall, no. He can't vote on a referendum on whether to boot him out of office.'

'What about the judge?' Starr asked.

'It's going to take a little longer to get rid of him, but we have begun working on the impeachment papers. I think we can show judicial malfeasance. Meanwhile, he wouldn't dare interfere with the special election. They'd probably string him up.'

'Today seems a little hasty to hold the election,' Chad said.

'Does it?' Hicks asked with surprise. It was Chad who had wanted to charge ahead with matters. 'The sooner the better. There are men gathering – strangers who look like they've been brought in to interfere with the election.'

'If you're talking about the men on the corners wearing red kerchiefs,' Chad told Hicks, 'they're cowboys from Wagonwheel. Art Spykes sent them over as special deputies.'

'Is that who they are?' Hicks said with a smile of relief. 'I thought I recognized Corey Bates. I once did some business for him in the matter of a stolen horse. They'll help keep a lid on things, but they aren't the men I was talking about. There must be ten or even twenty men gathered behind the Barbarossa stable. I recognized a couple of them, but I don't know their names. They're all Walker riders, that's all I know.'

Both Chad and Starr tensed on hearing this news. Starr had already walked to the rifle rack, had already withdrawn a box of cartridges from the desk drawer. It was time. They hadn't had to do a lot of fighting since they had been hired. Now it seemed that their time had come.

'Better get out and spread some of these around,' Chad said, thumping a finger on the bulletin on his desk. 'We'll want the citizens on our side as well.'

'I've got half a dozen boys ready to deliver them to all the shops, the saloons. We're just waiting for the printer to finish the batch. Then he's going to start on the ballots.'

'I'm grateful to you, Hicks. We couldn't have gotten this far without you.'

'It's my town too,' Reg Hicks said. 'Now, if you'll excuse me, I'd better get back over to the print shop.'

'We're in for it,' Starr said, tossing a rifle to Chad. 'How do you want to handle it?'

'First we let Hicks's boys deliver their bulletins. Then, if anything starts up, the people in this town will have an idea what it's all about.'

'I'm not very good at waiting,' Starr said.

Chad grinned. 'And I'm not very good at rushing ten or more men and trying to disarm them.'

Starr sat on the desk, Winchester on his knees. 'I guess I shouldn't be surprised that Glen Walker already knew what was happening.'

'I told you once, Glen Walker knows everything that goes on in this town. He might have gotten the word from a Wagonwheel man, it might have been a printer's devil, someone in the house of Councilman Kennedy or Walsh. Who knows? Everyone knows that Glen Walker is willing to pay for any useful information.'

'And he wasn't just bragging when he said he could call in a dozen armed men anytime he wanted to.'

'No,' Chad said heavily. 'He wasn't just bragging about that.'

If the Wagonwheel riders just held their positions they were forming a sort of safe corridor through which voters could pass on their way to the court-house. Chad had no idea what Walker's plan of action was; he only knew that by now the town manager must be in a furious mood. He was paying a lot of men a lot of money for a very dangerous job. At least one man would be charged with eliminating

Chad Dempster, of that he was sure.

They had kept the door to the jailhouse closed, but an hour after Reg Hicks's visit they could look out of the window and see five or six boys between the ages of eleven and fourteen fanning out across the town, sheaves of bulletins under their arms. They went into the Silver Eagle, the Clipper, the FitzRoy and every shop in between: haberdashers, dressmakers, the candy store, the blacksmith's shop, the general store, hardware emporium, boot-maker's, gunsmith, stables, feed-and-grain store. Not missing any place of business.

It didn't take long to start a reaction. Half an hour later men and women from all the various businesses could be seen walking along Main Street in the direction of the courthouse.

'Now it's going to start,' Byron Starr said soberly. 'We'd better get out there and keep an eye on things, Chad.'

He was right. Almost before he had finished speaking they heard a shot ring out. Another answered it. Up the street to the west they could see a band of Glen Walker riders walking up the street. A man with a red kerchief lay sprawled in the dust and one of the marchers was limping badly.

'Let's cut across the street,' Chad said. 'Those Wagonwheel cowboys are going to open up.'

With one of their own shot down, that indeed was what they did. All along the street the men with the red scarves opened up from places of concealment, behind water barrels and from alleyways. Glen Walker's thugs were forced to dive for whatever cover they could find.

Chad saw another Wagonwheel cowboy take a shot in the leg and be spun around only to steady himself and fire back at the Walker men, catching one of them in the chest. The Walker rider howled and hit the ground face first. There was no one to drag him out of the street. All of his friends had rushed toward cover and were now firing back furiously at the Wagonwheel crew.

Two of the Walker men tried to take shelter in the FitzRoy saloon, but Chad heard the roar of the barkeep's shotgun and saw one of them turn away to fall on the boardwalk while the other took to his heels, diving for the alley entrance.

'Come on!' Chad shouted to Starr. 'We'd better keep moving.'

Starr's answer was a panting question as they rushed up the alley beside Meyer the blacksmith's open-air forge. 'Where are we going?'

'The back of the Barbarossa stable – that's where they left their horses,' Chad said, pausing as Starr slowed and caught up with him at a walk.

'Chad,' Starr said sincerely, 'you don't want to do that.'

'It's where they'll run if the Wagonwheel men beat them back.'

'Exactly,' Starr said. He was bent over at the waist, trying to suck air into his lungs. Starr was obviously not in shape for sprinting. 'Tell me, Chad, what do you want these men to do?'

'I want them out of my town,' Chad said angrily.

'That's right,' Starr commented. 'That's what I want, too. But if we cut them off from their ponies, they'll have no choice but to fight to the last man. Don't you see? Let them have their horses.'

Chad pondered this for only a few seconds before he nodded and said, 'You're right, Starr. In that case, we'd better get back to Main Street and see if we can help out the Wagonwheel men.'

They turned then and started back toward the center of town where the guns still fired continuously. There was a lot of ammunition being burned in the streets of Las Palmas on this morning.

Four or five strides on he stepped out of the shadows.

Glen Walker's expression was wolfish, his eyes glittering. He still wore his ivory-colored suit, his scarlet cravat, but the tie was disarranged, the suit smudged badly. There was a pistol in his hand and he held it with deadly intent.

'You interfering snake. You ungrateful stumble-bum,' he said as he braced himself not far from Meyer's glowing forge. 'You've ruined everything.'

He gave no other warning, Chad saw Glen Walker thumb back the hammer of his Colt, and Chad drew as rapidly as he could. Still it seemed he was moving under water, his movements in slow dream-time as he pulled his own pistol from its holster and fired. A distant roar overwhelmed his ears and sudden violent pain coursed through his shoulder as if red-hot iron from Meyer's forge had been run through his body.

He felt his knees come undone. They buckled and he fell to the ground, sprawled against the oily sand of the alley. The sun was in his eyes when he opened them, a piercing desert sun. His legs had begun to twitch uncontrollably.

Starr was beside him on his knees, bent over him, trying to do something with his yellow bandanna. Chad tried to smile, but it hurt. He only had enough strength to ask:

'Glen Walker?'

'He's dead,' Starr told him, trying to stanch the blood with his bandanna.

'Thanks, Starr . . . I knew you'd get him.'

'I didn't get him, Chad. You did. I guess that practice paid off in the end.'

TWELVE

The sun peering in the window awakened Chad Dempster. He blinked into the light. He had to get to work. He then realized that the sun was much too high. How late was he? Poor Starr would be left holding down the office. He started to swing his feet to the floor and found that he could not move them. The pain that followed that attempt brought back with it the memory of the alley fight, the attempt to save the town. But the memory was spotty. He could not remember all that had gone on, so he closed his eyes again and lay back, his half-dreams haunted by shadowy men with guns.

Sometime later he heard the door to his bedroom squeak open and he squinted up to see Candida standing there, a questioning look on her face.

'You know me?' she asked.

'Of course I do,' Chad answered with a smile.

'I am sorry. This is the first time you have known me,' she said.

'What do you mean?'

'All of this week you did not know anyone who came to see you.'

'A week!' Chad said, startled to alertness. 'It can't have been.'

'Yes, it has been. You would eat – eagerly – and sit up to drink water, but you did not know anybody.' She sat on the foot of his bed. The sunlight gleamed on her raven-black hair, highlighting it. 'You were shot very bad.'

'I thought you'd run away from me,' Chad said, 'when I didn't see you here.'

'I thought of running away. I was staying away because I did not wish to see what was bound to happen to you. I thought it would make it easier if I did not see you dead.' She shook her head. 'But it did not.'

'Now . . . will I be seeing you again, Candida? Or will you go?' he asked weakly.

'I will stay,' she said, rising. 'Then we must do some very serious talking about what we should do.'

Chad nodded, but his head fell back again and his eyelids closed, too heavy to hold open. He tried to remember what Candida had said, what the implications might have been, but he could not hold onto the thoughts, and he fell away back into the world where masked gunmen appeared from every direction, firing their pistols at him.

Later that afternoon, or was it the following afternoon? – time had ceased to have any meaning for him – Chad awakened to find Byron Starr sitting on a reversed wooden chair beside his bed, hat tilted back on his head.

'I heard you were awake and alert, so I thought I'd swing by,' Starr said.

'I'm awake,' Chad said. 'As far as being alert, well, I don't know about that. How's everything in town?'

'Better, much better. Things have calmed down considerably in Las Palmas.'

'Glad to hear it. I'm sorry I can't give you any help just now. You must need it.'

'We're doing all right,' Starr said. 'I got me a new deputy. No experience. He just stepped down from the stage in Las Palmas, said he'd stopped here because he had run out of money and couldn't travel on any further. I told him I'd give him a try. Didn't even have a gun or know how to shoot one. I gave him a few tips. I think he'll work out fine.'

'Did you give him the night shift?' Chad asked.

'Yes, I did.' Starr smiled. 'Peggy is through with all that night work. We've got a little room in a house off Nopal Street. Still saving to buy a house of our own.'

'Sounds like you're doing fine,' Chad said. 'I guess we can go to eight-hour shifts once I'm up again.'

'What in the world do you need with two jobs?' Starr asked, smiling again.

'I don't get you,' Chad said, forcing himself to sit up straighter in bed.

'No one told you?' Starr asked. 'Maybe they did and you were too groggy to understand.'

'Understand what?' Chad's mockingbird had come back to perch on the ledge and cock its head, looking in at the two men.

'Why, Chad, you were elected mayor of Las Palmas in the recent election. Reg Hicks told me that he had to put the ballots together quickly, and he put you down only to fill out the choice of candidates.

'The thing was, everyone knew your name, about the fight in Lone Pine, about the shooting of Domino Jones, the saloon brawl when you took out Deacon Forge and Skinny Jim by yourself, about your part in trying to shut down Glen Walker and his cronies. Why, you were swept in to office. You're a regular local hero, Chad.'

'Half of what people know about me is malarkey,' Chad grumbled.

'Yes,' Starr said, rising. 'That's what's called politics. Anyway, the day before yesterday I saw former-Mayor Swanson and Judge Lambert climbing aboard the afternoon stage. I waved them on their way. It was a fine feeling.'

'Really, we owe all this to Reg Hicks. Without him

none of this would have happened. I'll have to thank him.'

'As soon as he gets back, I'm sure he'd appreciate that,' Starr said.

'Gets back? What did he do, go up to the territorial capital about matters?'

'Not exactly. It's more of a pleasure trip. He and his wife left on their honeymoon.'

'He got married! To whom? Anyone I might know?'

'It was Carmalita,' Starr said with a grin. 'It's amazing, but women like her always seem to land on their feet.'

'Carmalita! How could. . . ?' But Chad had already heard enough to absorb and come to terms with, and his eyes were very heavy. He hardly heard the door close when Starr slipped out of the room.

One month later most of Las Palmas came to see their mayor and Candida wed at the small church. Marshal Starr and Peggy Kimball were in attendance, as were Reg Hicks, the newly appointed judge, with his wife, Carmalita. The aunts in Spanish costumes sat solemnly in the front pew. Ben Cody had made the trip over from his house along with Art Spykes, a hard-eyed, sun-toasted man. Kennedy and Walsh from the city council showed up along with the owners of the Clipper, Silver Eagle and FitzRoy saloons. The banker, Sam Pettit and his brother, Walter, from Diablo were there. There were so many others from around town that there was standing room only in the back of the church.

Chad was still feeling a little stiff and awkward in his movements, but he had insisted that they follow through with the wedding plans. On his way up the steps to the altar he stumbled a little until Candida caught his arm and straightened him up. There was not the slightest snicker from those assembled as Tanglefoot gathered himself and continued on his way to stand up before the preacher.